F. Marion Crawford

Love in idleness - a tale of Bar Harbour

With illustrations reproduced from drawings and photographs

F. Marion Crawford

Love in idleness - a tale of Bar Harbour
With illustrations reproduced from drawings and photographs

ISBN/EAN: 9783743302938

Manufactured in Europe, USA, Canada, Australia, Japa

Cover: Foto ©Andreas Hilbeck / pixelio.de

Manufactured and distributed by brebook publishing software
(www.brebook.com)

F. Marion Crawford

Love in idleness - a tale of Bar Harbour

A Tale of Bar Harbour

BY

F. MARION CRAWFORD

AUTHOR OF " MR. ISAACS," "SARACINESCA," " KATHARINE
LAUDERDALE," ETC.

*WITH ILLUSTRATIONS REPRODUCED FROM DRAWINGS
AND PHOTOGRAPHS*

New York

MACMILLAN AND CO.

AND LONDON

1894

Norwood Press:
J. S. Cushing & Co. — Berwick & Smith.
Boston. Mass.. U.S.A.

LOVE IN IDLENESS.

CHAPTER I.

'M going to stay with the three Miss Miners at the Trehearnes' place," said Louis Lawrence, looking down into the blue water as he leaned over the rail of the *Sappho*, on the sunny side of the steamer. "They're taking care of Miss Trehearne while her mother is away at Karlsbad with Mr. Trehearne," he added, in further explanation.

"Yes," answered Professor Knowles, his companion. "Yes," he repeated vaguely, a moment later.

"It's fun for the three Miss Miners, having such a place all to themselves for the summer," continued young Lawrence. "It's less amusing for Miss Trehearne, I daresay. I suppose I'm

Sappho.

asked to enliven things. It can't be exactly gay in their establishment."

"I don't know any of them," observed the Professor, who was a Boston man. "The probability is that I never shall. Who are the three Miss Miners, and who is Miss Trehearne?"

"Oh — you don't know them!" Lawrence's voice expressed his surprise that there should be any one who did not know the ladies in question. "Well — they're three old maids, you know."

"Excuse me, I don't know. Old maid is such a vague term. How old must a maid be, to be an old maid?"

"Oh — it isn't age that makes old maids. It's the absence of youth. They're born so."

"A pleasing paradox," remarked the Professor, his exaggerated jaw seeming to check the uneasy smile, as it attacked the gravity of his colourless thin lips.

His head, in the full face view, was not too large for his body, which, in the two dimensions of length and breadth, was well proportioned. The absence of the third dimension, that is, of bodily thickness, was very apparent when he was seen sideways, while the exaggeration of the skull was also noticeable only in profile. The forehead and the long delicate jaw were

unnaturally prominent; the ear was set much
too far back, and there was no develop-
ment over the eyes, while the nose was small,
thin, and sharp, as though cut out of letter
paper.

"It's not a paradox," said Lawrence, whose
respect for professorial statements was small.
"The three Miss Miners were old maids before
they were born. They're not particularly old,
except Cordelia. She must be over forty.
Augusta is the youngest — about thirty-two, I
should think. Then there's the middle one —
she's Elizabeth, you know — she's no particular
age. Cordelia must have been pretty — in a
former state. Lots of brown hair and beautiful
teeth. But she has the religious smile — what
they put on when they sing hymns, don't you
know? It's chronic. Good teeth and resigna-
tion did it. She's good all through, but you
get all through her so soon! Elizabeth's clever
— comparatively. She's brown, and round, and
fat, and ugly. I'd like to paint her portrait.
She's really by far the most attractive. As for
Augusta — "

"Well? What about Augusta?" enquired the Professor, as Lawrence paused.

"Oh — she's awful! She's the accomplished one."

"I thought you said that the middle one — what's her name? — was the cleverest."

"Yes, but cleverness never goes with what they call accomplishments," answered the young man. "I've heard of great men playing the flute, but I never heard of anybody who was 'musical' and came to anything — especially women. Fancy Cleopatra playing the piano — or Catherine the Great painting a salad of wild flowers on a fan! Can you? Or Semiramis sketching a lap dog on a cushion!"

"What very strange ideas you have!" observed the Professor, gravely.

Lawrence did not say anything in reply, but looked out over the blue water at the dark green islands or the deep bay as the *Sappho* paddled along, beating up a wake of egg-white froth. He was glad that Professor Knowles was going over to the other side to dwell amongst the placid inhabitants of North East Harbour, where the joke dieth not, even at an advanced age; where there are people who believe in Ruskin and swear by Herbert Spencer, who coin words ending in 'ism,' and intellectually subsist on the 'ologies'—with the notable exception of theology. Lawrence had once sat at the Professor's feet, at Harvard, unwillingly, indeed, but not without indirect profit. They had met to-day in the train, and it was not probable that they should meet again in the course of the summer, unless they particularly sought one another's society.

They had nothing in common. Lawrence was an artist, or intended to be one, and had recently returned from abroad, after spending three years in Paris. By parentage he belonged to New York. He had been christened Louis because his mother was of French extraction and had an uncle of that name, who might be expected to do something handsome for her son. Louis Lawrence was now about five and twenty years of age, was possessed of considerable talent, and of no particular worldly goods. His most important and valuable possession, indeed, was his

character, which showed itself in all he said and
did.

There is something problematic about the
existence of a young artist who is in earnest,
which alone is an attraction in the eyes of
women. The odds are ten to one, of course,
that he will never accomplish anything above
the average, but that one-tenth chance is not to
be despised, for it is the possibility of a well-
earned celebrity, perhaps of greatness. The one
last step, out of obscurity into fame, is generally
the only one of which the public knows anything,
sees anything, or understands anything; and no
one can tell when, if ever, that one step may be
taken. There is a constant interest in expecting
it, and in knowing of its possibility, which lends
the artist's life a real charm in his own eyes
and the eyes of others. And very often it turns
out that the charm is all the life has to recom-
mend it.

The young man who had just given Professor
Knowles an account of his hostesses was naturally inclined to be communicative, which is a
weakness, though he was also frank, which is

a virtue. He was a very slim young man, and might have been thought to be in delicate health, for he was pale and thin in the face. The features were long and finely chiselled, and the complexion was decidedly dark. He would have looked well in a lace ruffle, with flowing curls. But his hair was short, and he wore rough grey clothes and an unobtrusive tie. The highly arched black eyebrows gave his expression strength, but the very minute, dark mustache which shaded the upper lip was a little too evidently twisted and trained. That was the only outward sign of personal vanity, however, and was not an offensive one, though it gave him a foreign air which Professor Knowles disliked, but which the three Miss Miners thought charming. His manner pleased them, too; for he was always just as civil to them as though they had been young and pretty and amusing, which is more than can be said of the majority of modern youths. His conversation occasionally shocked them, it is true; but the shock was a mild one and agreeably applied, so that they were willing to undergo it frequently.

Lawrence was not thinking of the Miss Miners as he watched the dark green islands. If he had thought of them at all during the last half-hour, it had been with a certain undefined gratitude to them for being the means of allowing

him to spend a fortnight in the society of Fanny Trehearne.

Professor Knowles had not moved from his side during the long silence. Lawrence looked up and saw that he was still there, his extraordinary profile cut out against the cloudless sky.

"Will you smoke?" enquired Lawrence, offering him a cigarette.

"No, thank you — certainly not cigarettes," answered the Professor, with a superior air. "You were telling me all about the Miss Miners," he continued; for though he knew none of them, he was of a curious disposition. "You spoke of a Miss Trehearne, I think."

"Yes," answered the young man. "Do you know her?"

"Oh, no. It's an unusual name, that's all. Are they New York people?"

Lawrence smiled at the idea that any one should ask such a question.

"Yes, of course," he answered. "New York — since the Flood."

"And Miss Trehearne is the only daughter?" enquired the Professor, inquisitively.

"She has a brother — Randolph," replied Lawrence, rather shortly; for he was suddenly aware that there was no particular reason why he should talk about the Trehearnes.

"Of course, they're relations of the Miners," observed the Professor.

" That's the reason why Miss Trehearne has them to stay with her. Excuse me — I can't get a light in this wind."

Thereupon Lawrence turned away and got under the lee of the deck saloon, leaving the Professor to himself. Having lighted his cigarette, the artist went forward and stood in the sharp head-breeze that seemed to blow through and through him, disinfecting his whole being from the hot, close air of the train he had left half an hour earlier.

Bar Harbour, in common speech, includes Frenchman's Bay, the island of Mount Desert, and the other small islands lying near it, — an extensive tract of land and sea. As a matter of fact, the name belongs to the little harbour between Bar Island and Mount Desert, together with the village which has grown to be the centre of civilization, since the whole place has become fashionable. Earth, sky, and water are of the north, — hard, bright, and cold. In artists' slang, there is no atmosphere. The dark green islands, as one looks at them, seem to be almost before the foreground. The picture is beautiful,

and some people call it grand; but it lacks
depth. There is something fiercely successful
about the colour of it, something brilliantly self-
reliant. It suggests a certain type of handsome
woman — of the kind that need neither repent-
ance nor cosmetics, and are perfectly sure of the
fact, whose virtue is too cold to be kind, and
whose complexion is not shadowed by passion,
nor softened by suffering, nor even washed pale
with tears. Only the sea is eloquent. The
deep-breathing tide runs forward to the feet of
the over-perfect, heartless earth, to linger and
plead love's story while he may; then sighing
sadly, sweeps back unsatisfied, baring his deso-
late bosom to her loveless scorn.

The village, the chief centre, lies by the
water's edge, facing the islands which enclose
the natural harbour. It was and is a fishing
village, like many another on the coast. In the
midst of it, vast wooden hotels, four times as high
as the houses nearest to them, have sprung up
to lodge fashion in six-storied discomfort. The
effect is astonishing; for the blatant architect,
gesticulating in soft wood and ranting in paint,

Old Indian Village.

as it were, has sketched an evil dream of mediæ-valism, incoherent with itself and with the very commonplace facts of the village street. There, also, in Mr. Bee's shop window, are plainly visible the more or less startling covers of the newest books, while from on high, frowns down the counterfeit presentment of battlements and turrets, and of such terrors as lent like interest when novels were not, neither was the slightest idea of the short story yet conceived.

But behind all and above all rise the wooded hills, which are neither modern nor ancient, but eternal. And in them and through them there is secret sweetness, and fragrance, and much that is gentle and lovely — in the heart of the defiantly beautiful earth-woman with her cold face, far beyond the reach of her tide-lover, and altogether out of hearing of his sighs and com-plaining speeches. There grow in endless green-ness the white pines and the pitch pines, the black spruce and the white; there droops the feathery larch by the creeping yew, and there gleam the birches, yellow, white, and grey; the sturdy red oak spreads his arms to the scarlet maple, and the witch hazel rustles softly in the mysterious forest breeze. There, buried in the wood's bosom, bloom and blossom the wild

flowers, and redden the blushing berries in unseen succession, from middle June to late September — violets first, and wild iris, straw-berries and raspberries, blueberries and black-

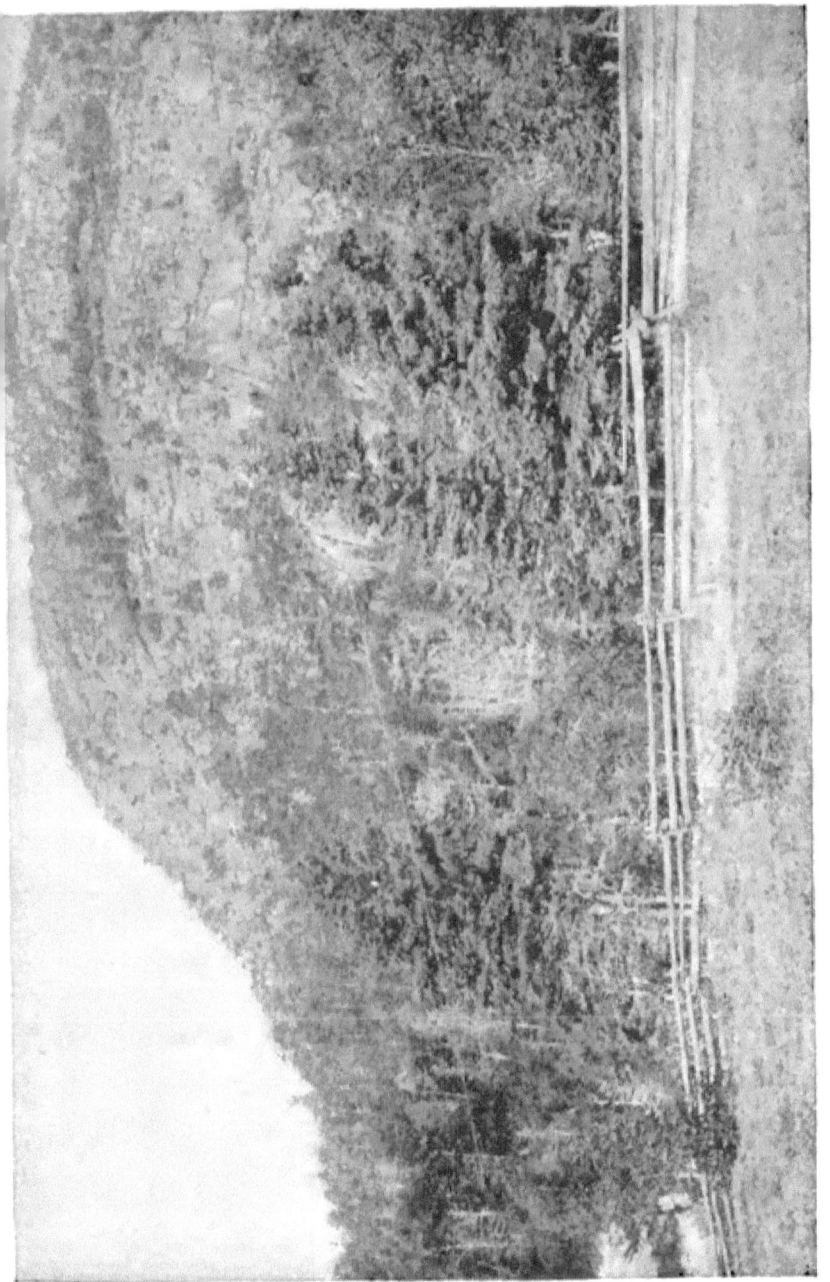

Beehive Mountain.

C

berries; short-lived wild roses and tender little blue-bells, red lilies, golden-rod, and clematis, in the confusion of nature's loveliest order.

All this Lawrence knew, and remembered, guessing at what he could neither remember nor know, with an artist's facility for filling up the unfinished sketch left on the mind by one impression. He had been at Bar Harbour three years earlier, and had wandered amongst the woods and pottered along the shore in a skiff. But he had been alone then and had stopped in the mediæval hotel, a rather solitary, thinking unit amidst the horde of thoughtless summer nomads, designated by the clerk at the desk as 'Number a hundred and twenty-three,' and a candidate for a daily portion of the questionable dinner at the hotel table. It was to be different this time, he thought, as he watched for the first sight of the pier when the *Sappho* rounded Bar Island. The Trehearnes had not been at their house three years ago, and Fanny Trehearne had been then not quite sixteen, just groping her way from the schoolroom to the world, and quite beneath his young importance — even had she been at Bar Harbour to wander among the woods with him. Things had changed, now. He was not quite sure that in her girlish heart she did not consider him beneath her notice. She was straight and tall — almost as tall as he, and she was proud, if she was not pretty, and she carried her head as high as the handsomest. Moreover, she was rich, and Louis Lawrence was at present phenomenally poor, with a rather distant chance of inheriting money. These were some of the excellent reasons why fate had made him fall in love with her, though none of them accounted for the fact that she had encouraged him, and had suggested to the Miss Miners that it would be very pleasant to have him come and stay a fortnight in July.

The *Sappho* slowed down, stopped, backed, and made fast to the wooden pier, and as she swung round, Lawrence saw Fanny Trehearne standing a little apart from the group of people who had come down to meet their own friends or to watch other people meeting theirs. The young girl was evidently looking for him, and he took off his hat and waved it about erratically to

attract her attention. When she saw him, she
nodded with a faint smile and moved one step
nearer to the gangway, to wait until he should
come on shore with the crowd.

She had a quiet, business-like way of moving,
as though she never changed her position without a purpose. As Lawrence came along, trying
to gain on the stream of passengers with whom
he was moving, he kept his eyes fixed on her
face, wondering whether the expression would

change when he reached her and took her hand. When the moment came, the change was very slight.

"I like you — you're punctual," she said. "Come along!"

"I've got some traps, you know," he answered, hesitating.

"Well — there's the expressman. Give him your checks."

CHAPTER II.

HEY'VE all gone out in Mr. Brown's cat-boat — so I came alone," observed Miss Trehearne, when the expressman had been interviewed.

"Who are 'all'?" asked Lawrence. "Just the three Miss Miners?"

"Yes. Just the three Miss Miners."

"I thought you might have somebody stopping with you."

"No. Nobody but you. Why do you say 'stopping' instead of 'staying'? I don't like it."

"Then I won't say it again," answered Lawrence, meekly. "Why do you object to it, though?"

"You're not an Englishman, so there's no

reason why you shouldn't speak English.   Here's
the buckboard.   Can you drive?"

"Oh—well—yes," replied the young man,
rather doubtfully, and looking at the smart little
turn-out.

Fanny Trehearne fixed her cool grey eyes on
his face with a critical expression.

"Can you ride?" she asked, pursuing her
examination.

"Oh, yes — that is — to some extent.   I'm not
exactly a circus-rider, you know -- but I can get
on."

"Most people can do that.   The important
thing is not to come off.   What can you do —
anyway?   Are you a good man in a boat?   You
see I've only met you in society.   I've never
seen you do anything."

"No," answered Lawrence.   "I'm not a good
man in a boat, as you call it — except that I'm
never sea-sick.   I don't know anything about
boats, if you mean sail-boats.   I can row a little
— that's all."

"If you could 'row,' as you call it, you'd
say you could 'pull an oar'—you wouldn't

talk about 'rowing.' Well, get in, and I'll drive."

There was not the least scorn in her manner, at his inability to do all those things which are to be done at Bar Harbour if people do anything at all. She had simply ascertained the fact as a measure of safety. It was not easy to guess whether she despised him for his lack of skill or not, but he was inclined to think that she did, and he made up his mind that he would get up very early, and engage a sailor to go out with him and teach him something about boats. The resolution was half unconscious, for he was really thinking more of her than of himself just then. To tell the truth, he did not attach so much importance to any of the things she had mentioned as to feel greatly humiliated by his own ignorance.

"After all," said Miss Trehearne, as Lawrence took his seat beside her, "it doesn't matter. And it's far better to be frank, and say at once that you don't know, than to pretend that you do, and then try to steer and drown one, or to drive and then break my neck. Only one rather wonders where you were brought up, you know."

"Oh — I was brought up somehow," answered Lawrence, vaguely. "I don't exactly remember."

"It doesn't matter," returned his companion, in a reassuring tone.

"No. If you don't mind, I don't."

Fanny Trehearne laughed a little, without looking at him, for she was intent upon what she was doing. It was a part of her nature to fix her attention upon whatever she had in hand — a fact which must account for a certain indifference in what she said. Just then, too, she was crossing the main street of the village, and there were other vehicles moving about hither and thither. More than once she nodded to an acquaintance, whom Lawrence also recognized.

"It's much more civilized than it was when I was here last," observed Lawrence. "There are lots of people one knows."

"Much too civilized," answered the young girl. "I'm beginning to hate it."

"I thought you liked society — "

"I? What made you think so?"

This sort of question is often extremely embar-rassing. Lawrence looked at her thoughtfully, and wished that he had not made his innocent remark, since he was called upon to explain it.

"I don't know," he replied at last. "Some-how, I always associate you with society, and dancing, and that sort of thing."

"Do you? It's very unjust."

"Well — it's not exactly a crime to like society, is it? Why are you so angry?"

"I wish you wouldn't exaggerate! It does not follow that I'm angry because you're not fair to me."

"I didn't mean to be unfair. How you take one up!"

"Really, Mr. Lawrence — I think it's you who are doing that!"

Miss Trehearne, having a stretch of clear road before her, gave her pair their heads for a moment, and the light buckboard dashed briskly up the gentle ascent. Lawrence was watching her, though she did not look at him, and he thought he saw the colour deepen in her sun-burnt cheek, although her grey eyes were as cool as ever. She was certainly not pretty, according to the probable average judgment of younger men. Lawrence, himself, who was an artist, wondered what he saw in her face to attract him, since he could not deny the attraction, and could not attribute it altogether to expression nor to the indirect effect of her character acting upon his imagination. He did not like to believe, either, that the charm was fictitious, and lay in a certain air of superior smartness, the result of good taste and plenty of money. Anybody could wear serge, and a more or less nautical hat and gloves, just in the fashionable degree of looseness or tightness, as the case might be. Anybody who chose had the right to turn up a veil over the brim of the aforesaid hat, and anybody who did so stood a good chance of being sunburnt. Moreover, as Lawrence well knew, there is a quality of healthy complexion which tans to a golden brown, very becoming when the grey eyes have dark lashes, but less so when, as in Fanny Trehearne's case, the lashes and brows are much lighter than the hair — almost white, in fact. It is not certain whether the majority of human noses turn up or down. There was, however, no doubt but that Fanny's turned up. It was also apparent that she had decidedly high cheek bones, a square jaw, and a large mouth, with lips much too even and too little curved for beauty. After all, her best points were perhaps her eyes, her golden-brown complexion, and her crisp, reddish brown hair, which twisted itself into sharp little curls wherever it was not long enough to be smoothed. With a little more regularity of feature, Fanny Trehearne might have been called a milkmaid beauty, so far as her face was concerned. Fortunately for her, her looks were above or below such faint praise. It was doubtful whether she would be said to have charm, but she had individuality, since those terms are in common use to express gifts which escape definition.

A short silence followed her somewhat indignant speech. Then, the road being still clear before her, she turned and looked at Lawrence. It was not a mere glance of enquiry, it was certainly not a tender glance, but her eyes lingered with his for a moment.

"Look here — are we going to quarrel?" she asked.

"Is there any reason why we should?" Lawrence smiled.

"Not if we agree," answered the young girl, gravely, as she turned her head from him again.

"That means that we shan't quarrel if I agree with you, I suppose," observed the young man.

"Well, why shouldn't you?" asked Fanny, frankly. "You may just as well, you know. You will in the end."

"By Jove! You seem pretty sure of that!" Lawrence laughed.

Fanny said nothing in reply, but shortened the reins as the horses reached the top of the hill. Lawrence looked down towards the sea. The sun was very low, and the water was turning from sapphire to amaranth, while the dark islands gathered gold into their green depths.

"How beautiful it is!" exclaimed the artist, not exactly from impulse, though in real enjoyment, while consciously hoping that his companion would say something pleasant.

Harbour with the Islands called Porcupines.

"Of course it's beautiful," she answered. "That's why I come here."

"I should put it in the opposite way," said Lawrence.

"How?"

"Why — it's beautiful because you come here."

"Oh — that's ingenious! You think it's my mission to beautify landscapes."

"I thought that if I said something pretty in the way of a compliment, we shouldn't go on quarrelling."

"Oh! Were we quarrelling? I hadn't noticed it."

"You said something about it a moment ago," observed Lawrence, mildly.

"Did I? You're an awfully literal person. By the bye, you know all the Miss Miners, don't you? I've forgotten."

"I believe I do. There's Miss Miner the elder — to begin with — "

"The oldest — since there are three," said Fanny, correcting him. "Yes — she's the one with the hair — and teeth."

D

"Yes, and Miss Elizabeth — isn't that her name? The plainest —"

"And the nicest. And Augusta — she's the third. Paints wild flowers and plays the piano. She's about my age, I believe."

"Your age! Why, she must be over thirty!"

"No. She's nineteen, still. She's got an anchor out to windward — against the storm of time, you know. She swings a little with the tide, though."

"I don't understand," said Lawrence, to whom nautical language was incomprehensible.

"Never mind. I only mean that she does not want to grow old. It's always funny to see a person of nineteen who's really over thirty."

Lawrence laughed a little.

"You're fond of them all, aren't you?" he asked, presently.

"Of course! They're my relation — how could I help being fond of them?"

"Oh — yes," answered Lawrence, vaguely. "But they really are very nice — people."

"Why do you hesitate?"

"I don't know. I couldn't say 'very nice

ladies,' could I ? And I shouldn't exactly say 'very nice women' — and 'very nice people' sounds queer, somehow, doesn't it ? "

" And you wouldn't say 'very nice old maids ' — "

" Certainly not ! "

" No. It wouldn't be civil to me, nor kind to them. The truth is generally unkind and usually rude. Besides, they love you."

" Me ? "

"Yes. They rave about you, and your looks, and your manners, and your conversation, and your talents."

" The dickens ! I'm flattered ! But it's always the wrong people who like one."

" Why the wrong people ? " asked Fanny Trehearne, not looking at him.

" Because all the liking in the world from people one doesn't care for can't make up for the not liking of the one person one does care for."

"Oh — in that way. It's rash to care for only one person. It's putting all one's eggs into one basket."

" What an extraordinary sentiment ! "

"I didn't mean it for sentiment."

"No — I should think not! Quite the contrary, I should say."

"Quite," affirmed Fanny, gravely.

"Quite?"

"Yes — almost quite."

"Oh — 'almost' quite?"

"It's the same thing."

"Not to me."

The young girl would not turn her attention from her horses, though in Lawrence's inexpert opinion she could have done so with perfect safety just then, and without impropriety. The most natural and innocent curiosity should have prompted her to look into his eyes for a moment, if only to see whether he were in earnest or not. He would certainly not have thought her a flirt if she had glanced kindly at him. But she looked resolutely at the horses' heads.

"Here we are!" she exclaimed suddenly.

With a sharp turn to the left the buckboard swept through the open gate, the off horse breaking into a canter which Fanny instantly checked.

The near wheels passed within a foot of the gatepost.

"Wasn't that rather close?" asked Lawrence.

"Why? There was lots of room. Are you nervous?"

"I suppose I am, since you say so."

"I didn't say so. I asked."

"And I answered," said Lawrence, tartly.

"How sensitive you are! You act as though I had called you a coward."

"I thought you meant to. It sounded rather like it."

"You have no right to think that I mean things which I haven't said," answered the young girl.

"Oh, very well. I apologize for thinking that what you said meant anything."

"Don't lose your temper — don't be a spoilt baby!"

Lawrence said nothing, and they reached the house in silence. Fanny was not mistaken in calling him sensitive, though he was by no means so nervous, perhaps, as she seemed ready to believe. She had a harsh way of saying things which, spoken with a smile, could not have given offence, and Lawrence was apt to attach real importance to her careless speeches. He felt himself out of his element from the first, in a place where he might be expected to do things in which he could not but show an awkward inexperience, and he was ready to resent anything like the suggestion that timidity was at the root of his ignorance, or was even its natural result.

His face was unnecessarily grave as he held out his hand to help Fanny down from the buckboard, and she neither touched it nor looked at him as she sprang to the ground.

"Go into the library, and we'll have tea," she said, without turning her head, as she entered the house before him. "I'll be down in a moment."

She pointed carelessly to the open door and went through the hall in the direction of the staircase. Lawrence entered the room alone.

The house was very large; for the Trehearnes were rich people, and liked to have their friends with them in considerable numbers. Moreover, they had bought land in Bar Harbour in days when it had been cheap, and had built their dwelling commodiously, in the midst of a big lot which ran down from the road to the sea. With the instinct of a man who has been obliged to live in New York, squeezed in, as it were, between tall houses on each side, Mr. Trehearne had given himself the luxury, in Bar Harbour, of a house as wide and as deep as he could possibly desire, and only two stories high.

The library was in the southwest corner of the house, opening on the south side upon a deep verandah from which wooden steps descended to the shrubbery, and having windows to the west, which overlooked the broad lawn. The latter was enclosed by tall trees. The winding avenue led in a northerly direction to the main road. At the east end of the house, the offices ran out towards the boundary of the Trehearnes' land, and beyond them, among the trees, there was a small yard enclosed by a lattice of wood eight or ten feet high.

The library was the principal room on the ground floor, and was really larger than the drawing-room which followed it along the line of the south verandah, though it seemed smaller from being more crowded with furniture. As generally happens in the country, it had become a sort of common room in which everybody preferred to sit. The drawing-room had been almost abandoned of late, the three Miss Miners being sociable beings, unaccustomed to magnificence in their own homes, and averse to being alone with it anywhere. They felt that the drawing-room was too fine for them, and by tacit consent they chose the library for their general trysting-place and tea camp when they were indoors. Mrs. Trehearne, who was, perhaps, a little too fond of splendour, would have smiled at the idea as she thought of her gorgeously brocaded reception rooms in New York; but Fanny had simple tastes, like her father, and agreed with her old-maid cousins in preferring the plain, dark woodwork, the comfortable leathern chairs, and the backs of the books, to the dreary wilderness of expensive rugs and unnecessary gilding which lay beyond. For the sake of coolness, the doors were usually opened between the rooms.

CHAPTER III.

THE weather was warm. By contrast with the cool air of the bay he had lately crossed, it seemed hot to Lawrence when he entered the library. Barely glancing at the room, he went straight to one of the doors which opened upon the verandah, and going out, sat down discontentedly in a big cushioned straw chair. It was very warm, and it seemed suddenly very still. In the distance he could hear the wheels of the buckboard in the avenue, as the groom took it round to the stables, and out of the close shrubbery he caught the sharp, dry sound of footsteps rapidly retreating along a concealed cinder path. The air scarcely stirred the creeper which climbed up one of the pillars of the verandah and festooned

its way, curtain-like, in both directions to the
opposite ends.   On his right he could see the
broad, sloping lawn, all shadowed now by the tall
trees beyond.   Without looking directly at it, he
felt that the vivid green of the grass was softened
and that there must be gold in the tops of the
trees.   The sensation was restful, but his eyes
stared vacantly at the deep shrubbery which
began at the foot of the verandah steps and
stretched away under the spruces at his left.

He was exceedingly discontented, though he
had just arrived, or, perhaps, for that very reason
among many other minor ones.   He had never
had any cause to expect from Fanny Trehearne
anything in the way of sentiment, but he was
none the less persuaded that he had a moral
right to look for something more than chaff and
good-natured hospitality, spiced with such vigor-
ous reproof as " don't be a spoilt baby."

The words rankled.   He was asking himself
just then whether he was a 'spoilt baby' or
not.   It was of great importance to him to know
the truth.   If he was a spoilt baby, of course
Miss Trehearne had a right to say so if she liked,

though the expression was not complimentary. But if not, she was monstrously unjust. He did not deny that the accusation might be well founded ; for he was modest as well as sensitive, and did not think very highly of himself at present, though he hoped great things for the future, and believed that he was to be a famous artist.

The more he told himself that he had no right to expect anything of Fanny, the more thoroughly convinced he became that his right existed, and that she was trampling upon it. She had ordered him into the library in a very peremptory and high-and-mighty fashion to wait for her, regardless of the fact that he had travelled twenty-four hours, and had acquired the prerogative right of the traveller to soap and water before all else. No doubt he was quite presentable, since the conditions of modern railways had made it possible to come in clean, or comparatively so, from a longish run. But the ancient traditions ought not to be swept out of the way, Louis thought, and the right of scrubbing subsisted still. She might at least have given him a hint as to the whereabouts of his room, since she had left him to himself for a quarter of an hour. She had not been gone four minutes yet, but Louis made it fifteen, and fifteen it was to be, in his estimation.

Presently he heard a man's footstep in the library behind him, and the subdued tinkling of a superior tea-service, of which the sound differs from the clatter of the hotel tea-tray, as the voice, say, of Fanny Trehearne differed in refinement from that of an Irish cook. But it irritated Lawrence, nevertheless, and he did not look round. He felt that when Fanny came down again, he intended to refuse tea altogether — presumably, by way of proving that he was not a spoilt baby after all. He crossed one leg over the other impatiently, and hesitated as to whether, if he lit a cigarette, it would seem rude to be smoking when Fanny should come, even though he was really in the open air on the verandah. But in this, his manners had the better of his impatience, and after touching his cigarette case in his pocket, in a longing way, he did not take it out.

At last he heard Fanny enter the room. There was no mistaking her tread, for he had noticed that she wore tennis shoes. He knew that she could not see him where he sat, and he turned his head towards the door expectantly. Again he heard the tinkle of the tea-things. Then there was silence. Then the urn began to hiss and sing . . . . was . . . . ng. It was clear that . . She could . . . no idea that he . sitting outside, as h. . . . thought she might have taken . . . . . for him. He listened . . . . the . . . her step again, but it did not come, and, oddly enough, his heart began to beat more quickly. But he did not move. He felt a ridiculous determination to wait until she began to be impatient and to move about and look for him. He could not have told whether it were timidity, or nervousness, or ill-temper which kept him nailed to his chair, and just then he would have scorned the idea that it could be love in any shape, though his heart was beating so fast.

Suddenly his straining ear caught the soft

rustle made by the pages of a book, turned deliberately and smoothed afterwards. She was calmly reading, indifferent to his coming or staying away — reading while the tea was drawing. How stolid she was, he thought. She was certainly not conscious of the action of her heart as she sat there. For a few moments longer he did not move. Then he felt he wished to see her, to see how she was sitting, and how really indifferent she was. But if he made a sound, she would look up and lay down her book even before he entered the room. The verandah had a floor of painted boards, — which are more noisy than unpainted ones, for some occult reason, — and he could not stir a step without being heard. Besides, his straw easy-chair would creak when he rose.

All at once he felt how very foolish he was, and he got up noisily, an angry blush on his young face. He reached the entrance in two strides and stood in the open doorway, with his back to the light. As he had guessed, Fanny was reading.

"Oh!" he ejaculated with affected surprise, as he looked at her.

She did not raise her eyes nor start, being evidently intent upon finishing the sentence she had begun.

"I thought you were never coming," she said, absently.

He was more hurt than ever by her indifference, and sat down at a little distance, without moving the light chair he had chosen. Fanny reached the foot of the page, put a letter she held into the place, closed the book upon it, and then at last looked up.

"Do you like your tea strong or weak?" she enquired in a business-like tone.

"Just as it comes — I don't care," answered Lawrence, gloomily.

"Then I'll give it to you now. I like mine strong."

"It's bad for the nerves."

"I haven't any nerves," said Fanny Trehearne, with conviction.

"That's curious," observed Lawrence, with fine sarcasm.

Fanny looked at him without smiling, since there was nothing to smile at, and then poured

E

out his tea. He took it in silence, but helped himself to more sugar, with a reproachful air.

"Oh — you like it sweet, do you?" said Fanny, interrogatively.

"Peculiarity of spoilt babies," answered Lawrence, in bitter tones.

"Yes, I see it is."

And with this crushing retort Fanny Trehearne relapsed into silence. Lawrence began to drink his tea, burnt his mouth with courageous indifference, stirred up the sugar gravely, and said nothing.

"I wonder when they'll get home," said Fanny, after a long interval.

"Are you anxious about them?" enquired the young man, with affected politeness.

"Anxious? No! I was only wondering."

"I'm not very amusing, I know," said Lawrence, grimly.

"No, you're not."

The blood rushed to his face again with his sudden irritation, and he drank more hot tea to keep himself in countenance. At that moment he sincerely wished that he had not come to Bar Harbour at all.

"You're not particularly encouraging, Miss Trehearne," he said presently. "I'm sure, I'm doing my best to be agreeable."

"And you think that I'm doing my best to be disagreeable? I'm not, you know. It's your imagination."

"I don't know," answered Lawrence, his face unbending a little. "You began by telling me that you despised me because I'm such a duffer at out-of-door things, then you told me I was a spoilt baby, and now you're proving to me that I'm a bore."

"Duffer, baby, and bore!" Fanny laughed. "What an appalling combination!"

"It is, indeed. But that's what you said —"

"Oh, nonsense! I wasn't as rude as that, was I? But I never said anything of the sort, you know."

"You really did say that I was a spoilt baby—"

"No. I told you not to be, by way of a general warning—"

"Well, it's the same thing—"

"Is it? If I tell you not to go out of the

room, for instance, and if you sit still—is it the
same thing as though you got up and went
out?"

"Why no—of course not!   How absurd!"

"Well, the other is absurd too."

"I'll never say again that women aren't logi-
cal," answered Lawrence, smiling in spite of
himself.

"No—don't.   Have some more tea."

"Thanks—I've not finished.   It's too hot to
drink."

Thereupon, his good temper returning, he
desisted from self-torture by scalding, and set
the cup down.   Fanny watched him, but turned
her eyes away as he looked up and she met his
glance.

"I'm so glad you've come," she said quietly.
"I've looked forward to it."

Perhaps she was a little the more ready to say
so, because she was inwardly conscious of having
rather wilfully teased him, but she meant what
she said.   Lawrence felt his heart beating again
in a moment.   Resting his elbow on his knees,
he clasped his hands and looked down at the

pattern of the rug under his feet. She did not realize how easily she could move him, not being by any means a flirt.

"It's nothing to the way I've looked forward to it," he answered.

She was silent, but he did not raise his head. He could see her face in the carpet.

"You know that, don't you?" he asked, in a low voice, after a few moments.

Unfortunately for his information on the subject, the butler appeared just then, announcing a visitor.

"Mr. Brinsley."

It was clear that the manservant had no option in the matter of admitting the newcomer, who was in the room almost before his name was pronounced.

"How do you do, Miss Trehearne?" he began as he came swiftly forward. "I'm tremendously glad to find you at home. You're generally out at this hour."

"Is that why you chose it?" asked Fanny, with a little laugh and holding out her hand. "Do you know Mr. Lawrence?" she continued,

by way of introducing the two men. "Mr. Brinsley," she added, for Louis's benefit.

Lawrence had risen, and he shook hands with
a good grace. But he hated Mr. Brinsley at
once, both because the latter had come inop-
portunely and because his own sensitive nature
was instantly and strongly repelled by the
man.

There was no mistaking Mr. Brinsley's Canadian accent, though he seemed anxious to make
it as English as possible, and Lawrence disliked
Canadians; but that fact alone could not have
produced the strongly disagreeable sensation of
which the younger man was at once conscious,
and he looked at the visitor in something like
surprise at the strength of his instantaneous
aversion. Brinsley, though dressed quietly, and
with irreproachable correctness, was a showy
man, of medium height, but magnificently made.
His wrists were slender, nervous, and sinewy, his
ankles — displayed to advantage by his low rus-
set shoes — were beautifully modelled, whereas
his shoulders were almost abnormally broad, and
the cords and veins moved visibly in his athletic

neck when he spoke or moved. The powerful muscles were apparent under his thin grey clothes, and Lawrence had noticed the perfect grace and strength of his quick step when he had entered. In face he was very dark, and his wiry, short black hair had rusty reflexions. His skin was tanned to a deep brown, and mottled, especially about the eyes, with deep shadows, in which were freckles even darker than the shadows themselves. His beard evidently grew as high as his cheek bones, for the line from which it was shaved was cleanly drawn and marked by the dark fringe remaining above. His mustache was black and heavy, and he wore very small, closely cropped whiskers like those affected by naval officers. He had one of those arrogant, vain, astute noses which seem to point at whatever the small and beady black eyes judge to be worth having.

At a glance, Lawrence saw that Brinsley was an athlete, and he guessed instantly that the man must be good at all those things which Louis himself was unable to do. He was a man to ride, drive, run, pull an oar, and beat everybody at tennis. But neither was that the reason why Lawrence hated him from the first. It had been the touch of his hard dry hand, perhaps, or the flash of the light in his small black eyes, or his self-satisfied and all-conquering expression. It was not easy to say. Possibly, too, Louis thought that Brinsley was his rival, and resented the fact that Fanny had betrayed no annoyance at the interruption.

But Brinsley barely vouchsafed Lawrence a glance, as the latter thought, and immediately sat himself down much nearer to Miss Tre-hearne and the tea-table than Louis, in his previous rage, had thought fit to do.

"Well, Miss Trehearne," said Brinsley, "how is Tim? Isn't he all right yet?"

"He's better," answered Fanny. "He had a bad time of it, but you can't kill a wire-haired terrier, you know. He wouldn't take the phosphate. I believe it was sweetened, and he hates sugar."

"So do I. Please don't give me any," he added quickly, watching her as she prepared a cup of tea for him.

Lawrence's resentment began to grow again. It was doubtless because Mr. Brinsley never took sugar that Fanny had seemed scornfully surprised at the artist's weakness for it.

CHAPTER IV.

LOUIS LAWRENCE was exceedingly uncomfortable during the next few minutes, and to add to his misery, he was quite conscious that he had nothing to complain of. It was natural that he should not know the people in Bar Harbour, excepting those whom he had known before, and that he should be in complete ignorance of all projected gaieties. Of course no one had suggested to the Reveres, for instance, to ask him to their dance; because they were Boston people, they did not know him, and nobody was aware that he was within reach. Besides, Louis Lawrence was a very insignificant personage, though he was well-connected, well-bred, and not ill-looking. He was just now a mere struggling artist, with no money except in the questionable future, and if he had talent, it was problematical, since he had not distinguished himself in any way as yet.

He remembered all these things, but they did not console him. In order not to seem rude, he made vague remarks from time to time, when something occurred to him to say, but he inwardly wished Brinsley a speedy departure and a fearful end. Fanny seemed amused and interested by the man's conversation, and she herself talked fluently. Now and then Brinsley looked at Lawrence, really surprised by the latter's ignorance of everything in the nature of sport, and possibly with a passing contempt which Lawrence noticed and proceeded to exaggerate in importance. The artist was on the point of asking Fanny's permission to go and find the room allotted to him, when a sound of women's voices, high and low, came through the open windows. There was an audible little confusion in the hall, and the three Miss Miners entered the library one after the other in quick succession.

"Oh, Mr. Brinsley!" exclaimed Miss Cordelia, the eldest, coming forward with a pale smile which showed many of her very beautiful teeth.

" Mr. Brinsley is here," said Miss Elizabeth, the ugly one, in an undertone to Miss Augusta, who possessed the accomplishments.

Then they also advanced and shook hands with much cordiality, the remains of which were promptly offered to Lawrence. Mr. Brinsley did not seem in the least overpowered by the sudden entrance of the three old maids. He smiled, moved up several chairs to the tea-table, and laughed agreeably over each chair, though Lawrence could not see that there was anything to laugh at. Brinsley's vitality was tremendous, and his manners were certainly very good, so that he was a useful person in a drawing-room. His assurance, if put to the test, would have been found equal to most emergencies. But on the present occasion he had no need of it. It was evidently his mission to be worshipped by the

Street in Village.

three Miss Miners and to be liked by Miss Trehearne, who did not like everybody.

"I'm sure we've missed the best part of your
visit," said Miss Cordelia.

"Oh, no," answered Brinsley, promptly. "I've
only just come — at least it seems so to me,"
he added, smiling at Fanny across the tea-
table.

Lawrence thought he must have been in the
room more than half an hour, but the sisters
were all delighted by the news that their idol
meant to stay some time longer.

"How nice it would be if everybody made such
speeches!" sighed Miss Augusta to Lawrence,
who was next to her. "Such a charming way of
making Fanny feel that she talks well! I'm sure
he's really been here some time."

"He has," answered Lawrence, absently and
without lowering his voice enough, for Brinsley
immediately glanced at him.

"We've been having such a pleasant talk about
the dogs and horses," said the Canadian, willing
to be disagreeable to the one other man present.
"I'm afraid we've bored Mr. Lawrence to death,

Miss Trehearne — he doesn't seem to care for those things as much as we do."

" I don't know anything about them," answered the young man.

" I'm afraid you'll bore yourself in Bar Harbour, then," observed Mr. Brinsley. " What can you find to do all day long ? "

" Nothing. I'm an artist."

" Ah ? That's very nice — you'll be able to go out sketching with Miss Augusta — long excursions, don't you know ? All day — "

" Oh, I shouldn't dare to suggest such a thing ! " cried Miss Augusta.

" I'm sure I should be very happy, if you'd like to go," said Lawrence, politely facing the dreadful possibility of a day with her in the woods, while Brinsley would in all likelihood be riding with Fanny or taking her out in a catboat.

But Miss Augusta paid little attention to him, so long as Brinsley was talking, which was most of the time. The man did not say anything worth repeating, but Lawrence knew that he was far from stupid in spite of his empty talk. At last Lawrence merely looked on, controlling his nervousness as well as he could and idly watching the faces of the party. Brinsley talked on and on, twisting to pieces the stem of a flower which he had worn in his coat, but which had unaccountably broken off.

Lawrence wondered whether Fanny, too, could be under the charm, and he watched her with some anxiety. There was something oddly inscrutable in the young girl's face and in her quiet eyes that did not often smile, even when she laughed. He had the strong impression, and he had felt it before, that she was very well able to conceal her real thoughts and intentions behind a mask of genuine frankness and straightforwardness. There are certain men and women who possess that gift. Without ever saying a word which even faintly suggests prevarication, they have a masterly reticence about what they do not wish to have known, whereby their acquaintances are sometimes more completely deceived than they could be by the most ingenious falsehood. Lawrence was quite unable to judge from Fanny's face whether she liked Brinsley or not, but he was wounded by a certain deference, if that word

F

be not too strong, which she showed for the man's opinion, and which contrasted slightly with the dictatorial superiority which she assumed towards Lawrence himself. He consoled himself as well as he could with the reflexion that he really knew nothing about dogs, horses, or boats, and that Brinsley was certainly his master in all such knowledge.

As an artist, he could not but admire the perfect proportions of the visitor, the strength of him, and the satisfactory equilibrium of forces which showed itself in his whole physical being; but as a gentleman he was repelled by something not easily defined, and as a lover he suspected a rival. He had not much right, indeed, to believe that Fanny Trehearne cared especially for him, any more than to predicate that she was in love with Brinsley. But, being in love himself, he very naturally arrogated to himself such a right without the slightest hesitation, and he boldly asserted in his heart that Brinsley was nothing but a very handsome 'cad,' and that Fanny Trehearne was on the verge of marrying him.

The conversation, meanwhile, was lively to the

ear, if not to the intelligence. It was amazing to see how the three spinsters flattered their darling at every turn. Miss Cordelia led the chorus of praise, and her sisters, to speak musically, took up the theme, and answer, and counter-theme of the fugue, successively, in many keys. There was nothing that Mr. Brinsley did not know and could not do, according to the three Miss Miners, or if there were anything, it could not be worth knowing or doing.

" You'll flatter Mr. Brinsley to death," laughed Fanny, "though I must say that he bears it well."

A faint shade of colour rose in Miss Cordelia's pale cheeks, indicative of indignation.

" Fanny ! " she cried reprovingly. " How rude you are! I'm sure I wasn't saying anything at all flattering."

" I only wish people would say such things to me, then," retorted the young girl.

" We're all quite ready to, I'm sure, Miss Tre-hearne," said Brinsley, smiling in a way that seemed to make his heavy dark mustache retreat outward, up his cheeks, like the whiskers of a cat when it grins.

Fanny looked round and met Lawrence's eyes.

" You seem to be the only one who is ready," she said, laughing again. " One isn't a crowd, as the little boys say."

" Where do you get such expressions, my dear child?" asked Cordelia. " I really think you've learned more slang since you've been here this summer, though I shouldn't have believed it possible!"

" There!" exclaimed Fanny, turning to Mr. Brinsley again. " That's the kind of flattery my relatives lavish on me from morning till night! As if you didn't all talk slang, the whole time!"

" Fanny!" protested Augusta, whose accomplishments made her sensitive and conscious. " How can you say so?"

" Well — dialect, if you like the word better. I'll prove it you. You all say ' won't ' and ' shan't ' — and most of you say ' I'd like ' — for instance — and Mr. Brinsley says ' ain't,' because he's English — "

" Well — what ought we to say?" asked

Augusta. "Nobody says 'I will not,' and all that."

"You ought to. It's dialect not to — and the absurd thing is that people who go in for writing books generally write out all the things you don't say, and write them in the wrong order. We say 'wouldn't you' — don't we? Well, doesn't that stand for 'would not you'? And yet they print 'would you not' — always. It's ridiculous. I read a criticism the other day on a man who had written a book and who wrote 'will not you' for 'won't you' and 'would not you' for 'wouldn't you' because he wanted to be accurate. You've no idea what horrid things the critic said of him — he simply stood on his hind legs and pawed the air! It's so silly! Either we should speak as we write, or write as we speak. I don't mean in philosophy — and things — the steam-engine and the descent of man, and all that — but in writing out conversations. But then, of course, nobody will agree with me — so I talk as I please."

"There's a great deal of truth in what you say, Miss Trehearne," observed Brinsley, assuming a

wise air. "Besides, I beg to differ from Miss
Miner, on one point — I venture to say that I
don't dislike your slang, if it's slang at all. It's
expressive, of its kind."

"At last!" cried Fanny, with a laugh. "I
get some praise — faint, but perceptible."

"Faint praise isn't supposed to be complimentary," observed Lawrence, laughing too.

"That's true," answered Fanny. "It's just the
opposite — the thing with a d—. I won't say
it on account of Cordelia. She'd all frizzle up
with horror if I said it — wouldn't you, dear?
There'd positively be nothing left of you — nothing but a dear little withered rose-leaf with a
dewdrop in the middle, representing your tears
for my sins!"

"I'm afraid so," answered Cordelia, with a
little accentuation of her tired smile.

It was not a disagreeable smile in itself,
except that it was perpetual and was the expression of patiently and cheerfully borne adversity,
rather than of any satisfaction with things in
general. For the lives of the three Miss Miners
had not been happy. Sometimes Fanny felt a

sincere and loving pity for the three, and especially for the eldest. But there were also times when Cordelia's smile exasperated her beyond endurance.

Mr. Brinsley rose to go, rather suddenly, after checking a movement of his hand in the direction of his watch.

"You're not going, surely!" cried one or two of the Miss Miners. "You're coming to dinner."

"Stay as you are," suggested Fanny, greatly to Lawrence's annoyance.

"You're awfully kind," answered the Canadian. "But I can't, to-night. I wish I could. I've asked several people to dine with me at the Kebo Valley Club. I'd cut any other engagement, to dine with you — indeed I would. I'm awfully sorry."

Many regrets were expressed that he could not stay, and the leave-taking seemed sudden to Lawrence, who stood looking on, still wondering why he disliked the man so much. At last he heard the front door closed behind him.

"Who is Mr. Brinsley?" he asked of Fanny

Trehearne, while the three Miss Miners were settling themselves again.

" Oh — I don't know. I believe he's a Canadian Englishman. He's very agreeable — don't you think so? "

" He's the most delightful man I ever met! " sighed Augusta Miner, before Lawrence had time to say anything.

" Did you notice his eyes, Mr. Lawrence? " asked Miss Elizabeth. " Don't you think they're beautiful? "

" Beautiful? Well — it depends," Lawrence answered with considerable hesitation, for he did not in the least know what to say.

" Oh, but it isn't his eyes, nor his conversation! " put in Cordelia, emphatically. " It is that he's such a perfect gentleman! You feel that he wouldn't do anything that wasn't quite — quite — don't you know? "

" I'm not sure that I do," replied Lawrence, in some bewilderment. " But I understand what you mean," he added confidently.

" My dear," said Augusta to her eldest sister, " all that is perfectly true, as I always say. But

those are not the things that make him the most
charming man I ever met. Oh dear, no! Ever
so many men one knows have good eyes, and
talk well, and are gentlemen in every way. I'm
sure you wouldn't have a man about if he wasn't
a gentleman. Would you?"

"Oh no — in a wider sense — all the men we
have to do with are, of course —"

"Well," argued Augusta, "that's just what I'm
telling you, my dear. It isn't those things. It
lies much deeper. It's a sort of refined appre-
ciation — an appreciative refinement — both, you
know. Now, the other day, do you remember?
— when I was playing that Mazurka of Chopin —
did you notice his expression?"

"But he always has that expression when anything pleases him very much," said Miss Elizabeth.

"Yes, I know. But just then, it was quite
extraordinary — there's something almost child-
like — "

"If you go on about Mr. Brinsley in this way
much longer, you'll all have a fit," observed
Fanny Trehearne.

"My dear," answered Cordelia, gravely, "do you know what a 'fit' means? Really, sometimes, you do exaggerate — "

"A fit means convulsions — what babies have, you know. They used to say it was brought on by looking at the moon."

Lawrence felt a strong inclination to laugh at this moment, but he controlled it, and only smiled. Then, to his considerable embarrassment, they all appealed to him, probably in the hope of more praise for Brinsley.

"Do tell us how he strikes you, Mr. Lawrence," said Cordelia.

"Yes, do!" echoed Elizabeth.

"Oh, please do!" cried Augusta, at the same moment.

"I should be curious to know what you think of him," said Fanny Trehearne.

"Well, really," stammered the unfortunate young man, "I've hardly seen him — I've not had time to form an opinion — you must know him, and you all like him, and — it seems to me — that settles it. Doesn't it?"

While Lawrence was speaking, Miss Cordelia

stooped and picked something up from the floor.
He noticed that it was the leafless stem of the
flower which Brinsley had been twisting in his
fingers. She did not throw it away, but her
hand closed over it, and Lawrence did not see
it again.

CHAPTER V.

LOUIS LAWRENCE had not been at Bar Harbour a week before he became fully aware — if indeed there had previously been any doubt on the subject in his mind — that he was very much in love with Fanny Trehearne. It became clear to him that, although he had believed himself to be in love once or twice before then, he had been mistaken, and that he had never known until the present time exactly what love meant. He was not even sure that he was pleased with the passion, or, at least, with the form in which it attacked him. Sensitive as he was, it 'took him hard,' as the saying is, and he felt that it had the better of him at every turn, and disposed of him in spite of himself at every hour of the day.

When he was alone he wondered why he had been asked to the house, and whether Mr. and Mrs. Trehearne, who were abroad, knew anything about it. He was a modest man, and was inclined to underestimate himself, so that it could never have occurred to him that Fanny Trehearne might have been strongly attracted by him during their acquaintance in town, and might have insisted that he should be asked to come and pass a fortnight. Moreover, Fanny lost no opportunity of impressing upon him that he was a great favourite with the three Miss Miners, and she managed to convey the impression that he had been asked chiefly to please them, though she never said so.

Meanwhile, however, it was evident that the three sisters were absorbed in Mr. Brinsley, and that when the latter was present they took very little notice of Lawrence. He laughed at the thought that the three old maids should all be equally in love with the showy Canadian, and he told himself that the thing was ridiculous; that they were merely enthusiastic women, — 'gushing' women, he called them in his thoughts, —

who were flattered by the diplomatic and unfail-
ing civilities of a man who was evidently in
pursuit of Fanny Trehearne.

For by this time he was convinced that Brinsley had made up his mind to marry Fanny if
he could; and he hated him all the more for it,
even to formulating wicked prayers for the
suitor's immediate destruction. The worst of
it was, that the man might possibly succeed.
A girl who will and can ride anything, who
beats everybody at tennis, and who is as good
as most men in a sail-boat, may naturally be
supposed to admire a man who does those things,
and many others, in a style bordering upon perfection. This same man, too, though not exactly
clever in an intellectual way, possessed at least
the gifts of fluency and tact, combined with
great coolness under all circumstances, so far
as Lawrence had observed him. It was hardly
fair to assert that he was dishonest because he
flattered the three Miss Miners, and occupied
himself largely in trying to anticipate their small-
est wishes. He did it so well as to make even
Fanny Trehearne believe that he liked them

for their own sakes, and that his intentions were disinterested and not directed wholly to herself. Of course she knew that he wished to marry her; but she was used to that. Two, at least, of several men who had already informed her that their happiness depended upon winning her, were even now in Bar Harbour, — presumably repeating that or a similar statement to more or less willing ears. As for Lawrence, he could not fairly blame Brinsley for his behaviour — he confessed in secret that he flattered the three Miss Miners himself, with small regard for unprejudiced truth. Besides, they were very kind to him. But he found it hard to speak fairly of Brinsley when alone with Fanny Trehearne.

"I don't like the man," he said, on inadequate provocation, for the twentieth time.

"I know you don't," answered Fanny, calmly, "but that's no reason for letting go of the tiller. Mind the boom! she's going about — no — it's of no use to put the helm up now. We've no way on — let her go! No — I don't mean that — oh, do give it to me!"

And thereupon Fanny, who was sitting forward of him on the weather side, stretched her long arm across him, pushing him back into his corner, and put the helm hard down with her left hand, while she hauled in the sheet as much as she could with her right, bending her head low to avoid the boom as it came swinging over.

Lawrence could not help looking down at her, and he forgot all about the boom, being far too little familiar with boating to avoid it instinctively, when he felt the boat going about. It came slowly, for there was little wind; and the catboat, having no way on to speak of, was in no hurry to right herself and go over on the other tack, — but just as the shadow of the sail warned him that something was coming, he looked up, and at the same instant received the blow full on his forehead, just above his eyes. He wore a soft, knitted woollen cap, which did not even afford the protection of a visor.

Fanny turned her head at once, for the blow had been audible, and she saw what had happened. Lawrence had raised his hand to his forehead instinctively.

"Are you hurt?" asked Fanny, quickly, keep-

Boat Wharves.

G

ing her eyes upon him, and still holding the helm
hard over so as to give the boat way.

Lawrence did not answer at once. He was
half stunned, and still covered his forehead with
his hand. The young girl looked at him intently, and there was an expression in her eyes
which he, at least, had never seen there — a sudden, scared light which had nothing to do with
fear.

" Are you hurt ? " she asked again, gently.

His delicate face grew suddenly pale, as the
blood, which had rushed up at first under the
shock of the blow, subsided as suddenly. Fanny
turned her eyes from him and looked ahead and
under the sail to leeward. She let out a little
more sheet, so that the boat could run very free ;
for the craft, like most catboats, had a weather
helm when the sheet was well aft, and Fanny
wanted her hands. Moreover, Lawrence was
now on the lee side with her, and the boat would
have heeled too far over with the wind abeam.
As soon as the sail drew properly, Fanny sat up
beside Lawrence, steering across him with her
left hand. With her right she could reach the

water, and she scooped up what she could in her hollow palm, wetting her sleeve to the shoulder as she did so, for the boat was gaining speed. She dashed the drops in his face.

"Are you hurt?" she asked a third time, drawing away his hand and laying her own wet one upon his forehead.

"Oh no," he answered faintly. "I'm not hurt at all."

She could tell by his voice that he was not speaking the truth, and a moment later, as he leaned against the side of the boat, his head fell back, and his lips parted in a dead faint.

There was no scorn in the young girl's face for a man who could faint so easily, as it seemed; but the scared look came into her eyes again, and without hesitation, still steering with her left hand, she passed her right arm round his neck and supported him. The breeze was almost in her face now, for she was looking astern, and she knew by the way it fanned her whether she was keeping the boat fairly before it.

Lawrence did not revive immediately, and it was fortunate that there was so little wind, or

Fanny might have got into trouble. She looked at him a moment longer and hesitated, for the position was a difficult one, as will be admitted. But she was equal to it and knew what to do. Letting his head fall back as it would, she withdrew her arm, let go the helm, and hauled in the sheet as the boat's head came up. As the boom came over toward Lawrence's head, she caught it and lifted it over him, hauled in the slack and made the sheet fast, springing forward instantly to let go the halliards. The gaff came rattling down, and she gathered in the bellying sail hastily and took a turn round everything with the end of the throat halliard, which chanced to be long enough — the gaskets were out of her reach, in the bottom of the boat.

There was little or no sea on, as the tide was near the turning, and the catboat was rocking softly to the little waves when Fanny came aft again. Lawrence's head was still hanging back, his lips were parted, and his eyes were half open, showing the whites in a rather ghastly way. With strong arms the young girl half lifted him, and let him gently down upon the cushions in the stern-sheets. Then she leaned over the side and wetted her handkerchief and laid it upon his bruised forehead. The cold water and the change of position brought him to himself.

He opened his eyes and looked up into her face as she bent over him. Then, all at once, he seemed to realize what had happened, and with an exclamation he tried to sit up. But she would not let him.

"Lie still a minute longer!" she said authoritatively. "You'll be all right in a little while."

"But it isn't anything, I assure you," he protested, looking about him in a dazed way. "Please let me sit up! I won't make a fool of myself again — it's only my heart, you know. It stops sometimes — it wasn't the knock."

"Your heart?" repeated Fanny, with greater anxiety than Lawrence might have expected. "You haven't got heart disease, have you?"

"Oh no — not so bad as that. It's all right now. It will begin to beat very hard presently — there — I can feel it — and then it will go on regularly again. It isn't anything. I fancy I smoke too much — or it's coffee — or something.

Please don't look as though you thought it were anything serious, Miss Trehearne. I assure you, it's nothing. Lots of people have it."

" It is serious. Anything that has to do with the heart is serious."

Lawrence smiled faintly.

" Is that a joke ? " he asked. " If it is, please let me sit up."

" No — that isn't a reason," answered Fanny, laughing a little, though her eyes were still grave. " You must lie still a little longer. You might faint again, you know. It must be dangerous to have one's heart behaving so strangely."

" Oh — I don't believe so."

" You don't believe so ? You mean that it's possible, but that you hope it won't stop ? Is that it ? "

" Oh — well — perhaps. But I don't think there's any real danger. Besides — if it did, it's easy, you know."

" What's easy ? "

" It's an easy death — over at once, in a flash. No lingering and last words and all that." He laughed.

Fanny Trehearne's sunburned cheeks grew pale under their tan, and her cool grey eyes turned slowly away from his face, and rested on the blue water.

"Please don't talk about such things!" she said in a tone that seemed hard to Lawrence.

"Are you afraid of death?" he asked, still smiling.

"I?" She turned upon him indignantly. "No — I don't believe that I'm much afraid of anything — for myself."

"You turned pale," observed the young man, raising himself on his elbow as he lay on the cushions, and looking at her. Her colour came back more quickly than it had gone.

"Did I?" she asked indifferently enough. "It's probably the sun. It's hot, lying here and drifting."

"No. It wasn't the sun," said Lawrence, with conviction. "You were thinking that somebody you are fond of might die suddenly. We were talking about death."

"What difference does it make whom I was thinking of?" She spoke impatiently now, still watching the water.

"It makes all the difference there is, that's all," answered Lawrence. "Won't you tell me?"

"No. Certainly not! Why should I? Look here — if you're well enough to talk, you're well enough to help me to get the sail up again."

"Of course I am — but —" Lawrence showed no inclination to move.

"But what? You're too lazy, I suppose." Fanny laughed. "Let me see your forehead — take your cap off," she added, with a change of tone.

Lawrence thrust the cap back, which did not help matters much, as his hair grew low and partially hid the bruise. The skin was not broken, but it was almost purple, and a large swelling had already appeared.

"It's too bad!" exclaimed Fanny, looking at it, as he bent down his head, and softly touching it with her ungloved hand. "Tell me — do you feel very weak and dizzy still? I was only laughing when I spoke of your helping me with the sail."

"Oh no!" answered Lawrence, cheerfully. "It aches a little, of course, but it will soon go off."

"And your heart?" asked Fanny, anxiously. "Is it all right now? You don't think you'll faint again, do you?"

"Not a bit."

"I'm not sure. You're very pale."

"I'm always pale, you know. It's my nature It doesn't mean anything. Some people are naturally pale."

"But you're not. You're dark, or brown, and not red, but you're not usually pale. I wish I had some whiskey, or something, to give you."

She looked round the boat rather helplessly, as though expecting to discover a remedy for his weakness.

"Please don't make so much of it," said Lawrence, in a tone which showed that he was almost annoyed by her persistence. "I assure you that I won't have such bad taste as to die on your hands before we get to land!"

Fanny rose to her feet and turned away from him with an impatient exclamation.

"Just keep the helm amidships while I get the sail up," she said, without looking at him, and stepping upon the seat which ran along the side, she was on the little deck in a moment, with both halliards in her hands.

Lawrence sprang forward to help her, forgetting what she had just told him to do.

"Do as I told you!" she exclaimed quickly and impatiently. "Do you know what the tiller is? Well, keep it right in the middle till I tell you to do something else."

"Don't be fierce about it," laughed Lawrence, obeying her.

But when she was not looking, he pressed one hand to his forehead with all his might, as though to drive out the pain, which increased with every minute.

Meanwhile, Fanny laid her weight to the halliards, and the sail went flapping up, throat and peak. The girl was very strong, and had been taught to handle a catboat when she had been a mere child, so that there was nothing extraordinary in her accomplishing unaided a little feat which would have puzzled many a smart young gentleman who fancies himself half a sailor.

CHAPTER VI.

I T chanced that on that evening Roger Brinsley was to dine with the Miss Miners. He was often asked, and he accepted as often as he could. As a matter of fact, he was not so much sought after elsewhere, as he was willing to let the four ladies believe, for there were people in Bar Harbour who shared Lawrence's distrust of him, while admitting that, so far as they could tell, it was quite unfounded. There was nothing against him. The men said that he played a good deal at the club, and remarked that he was a good type of the professional gambler, but no one ever said that he won too much. On the contrary, it was believed that he had lost altogether rather heavily during the six weeks since he had first appeared. He paid cheerfully, however, and was thought to be rich. Nevertheless, the men whose opinion was worth having did not like him. They wondered why the Miss Miners had him so often to the house, and whether there were not some danger that Fanny Trehearne might take a fancy to him.

It was very late when Fanny and Lawrence got home, for the catboat had been carried far up Frenchman's Bay during the time after the little accident, and it had been necessary to beat to windward for two hours against the rising tide in order to fetch the channel between Bar Island and Sheep Porcupine. The consequence was that the pair had scarcely time to dress for dinner after they reached the house.

Lawrence felt ill and tired, and was conscious that the swelling on his forehead was not beautiful to see. He was still dazed, and by no means himself, when he looked into the glass and knotted his tie. But though he might well have given an excuse and stayed in his room instead of going down to dinner, he refused to consider the possibility of such a thing even for a moment. He felt something just then which more than compensated him for his bruises and his wretched sensation of weakness.

The conversation, after the boat had got under way again, had languished, and had been so constantly interrupted by the often repeated operation of going about, that Lawrence had not succeeded in bringing it back to the point at which Fanny had broken it off when she had gone forward to hoist the sail. But he had more than half guessed what might have followed, and the reasonable belief that he might be right had changed the face of his world. He believed that Fanny had turned pale at the idea that his life was in danger.

One smiles at the simplicity of the thought, in black and white, by itself, just itself, and nothing more. Yet it was a great matter to Louis Lawrence, and as he looked at his bruised face in the glass he felt that he was too happy to shut himself up in his room for the evening, out of sight of the cool grey eyes he loved.

He had assuredly not meant to frighten Fanny

Canoeing in the Harbour.

when he had spoken, and he had been very far from inventing an imaginary ailment with which to excite her sympathy. The whole thing had come up unexpectedly as the result of the accident. Hence its value.

As often happens, the two people in the house who had been most hurried in dressing were the first down, and as Lawrence entered the library he heard Fanny's footstep behind him. He bowed as they came forward together to the empty fireplace. She looked at him critically before she spoke.

"You're badly knocked about. How do you feel?" There was a man-like directness in her way of asking questions, which was softened by the beauty of her voice.

"I feel — as I never felt before," answered Lawrence, conscious that his eyes grew dark as they met hers. "You told me something to-day — though you did not say it."

Fanny did not avoid his gaze.

"Did I?" she asked very gravely.

"Yes. Plainly."

"I am very sorry," she answered, with a little sigh, and turning from him at last.

II

"Are you taking it back?" Louis's voice trembled as he asked the question.

"Hush!"

Just then the voices of the three Miss Miners were heard in the hall, and at the same instant the distant tinkle of the front-door bell announced the arrival of Roger Brinsley.

The conversation turned upon Lawrence's accident, from the first, as was natural, considering his appearance. He dwelt laughingly on his utter helplessness in a boat, while Fanny was inclined to consider the whole affair as rather serious. For some reason or other Brinsley was displeased at it, and ventured to say a disagreeable thing. He had lost at cards in the afternoon, and was in bad humour. He spoke to Fanny with affected apprehension.

"You really ought to take somebody with you who knows enough to lend a hand at a pinch, Miss Trehearne," he said. "Suppose that you got into a squall and had to take a reef — you'd be in a bad way, you know."

"If I couldn't manage a catboat alone, I'd walk," answered Fanny, with contempt.

"Yes — no doubt. But if a squall really came up, what would you do? Mr. Lawrence confesses that he couldn't help you."

"Are you chaffing, Mr. Brinsley?" asked Fanny, severely. "Or do you think I really shouldn't know what to do?"

"I doubt whether you would."

"Oh — I'd let go the halliards and lash the helm amidships, and take my reef with the sail down — 'hoist 'em up and off again,' after that, as the fishermen say."

"I think you could stand an examination," said Brinsley.

"I daresay. Could you? If you were going about off a lee shore in a storm and missed stays, could you club-haul your ship, Mr. Brinsley?"

The three Miss Miners stared at the two in surprise and wonder, not understanding a word of what they were saying. It was apparent to Lawrence, however, that Fanny was bent on putting Brinsley in the position of confessing his ignorance at last; but where the young girl had learned even the language of seamanship, which she used with such apparent precision, was more than Lawrence could guess. Brinsley did not answer at once, and Fanny pressed him.

" Do you even know what club-hauling means ? " she asked, mercilessly.

" Well — no — really, I think the term must be obsolete."

" Not at sea," retorted Fanny.

This was crushing, and Brinsley, who was really a very good hand at ordinary sailing, grew angry.

" Of course you've had some experience in catboats," Fanny continued. " That isn't serious sailing, you know. It's about equivalent, in horsemanship, to riding a donkey — a degree less dignified than walking, and a little less trouble."

" I won't say anything about myself, Miss Trehearne," said Brinsley, " but you might treat the catboat a little less roughly. I didn't know you'd ever sailed anything else."

Here the Miss Miners interposed, one after the other, protesting that it was not fair to use up the opportunities of conversation in such nautical jargon.

"I only wished to prove to Mr. Brinsley that I'm to be trusted at sea," Fanny answered.

"My dear child," said Miss Cordelia, "Mr. Brinsley knows that, and he must be a good judge, having been in the navy."

"Oh, I didn't know you'd been in the navy, Mr. Brinsley," said the pitiless young girl, fixing her eyes on his with an expression which he, perhaps, understood, though no one else noticed it. "The English navy, of course?"

"The English navy," repeated Mr. Brinsley, sharply.

"Oh, well — that accounts for your not knowing how to club-haul a ship. Your own people are always saying that your service is going to the dogs."

Even Lawrence was surprised, and Brinsley looked angrily across the table at his tormentor, but found nothing to say on the spur of the moment.

"However," Fanny continued with some condescension, "I'm rather glad to know you're a navy man. I'll get you to come out with me some day and verify some of the bearings on our

local chart. I believe there are one or two mis-
takes. We'll take the sextant and my chronom-
eter with us, and the tables, and take the sun —
each of us, you know, and work it out separately,
and see how near we get. That will be great
fun. You must all come and see Mr. Brinsley
and me take the sun," she added, looking round
at the others. " Let's go to-morrow. We'll take
our luncheon with us and picnic on board. Can
you come to-morrow, Mr. Brinsley? We must
start at eleven so as to get far enough out to
have a horizon by noon. I hope you're not engaged? Are you?"

" I'm sorry to say I am," answered the unfortunate man. " I'm going to ride with some people just at that hour."

" How unlucky!" exclaimed Fanny, who had
expected the refusal. " I'll take Mr. Lawrence,
anyhow, and give him a lesson in navigation."

" I've had one to-day," said Lawrence, affecting
to laugh, for it was his instinct to try and turn
off any conversation from a disagreeable subject.

" You'll be all the better for another to-morrow," answered Fanny.

As she spoke to the artist, her tone changed so perceptibly that even the Miss Miners noticed it. Brinsley took the first opportunity of talking to Miss Cordelia, of whose admiration he was sure, and the rest of the dinner passed off in peace, Brinsley avoiding a renewal of hostilities with something almost like fear, for he felt that the extraordinary young girl who knew so much about navigation was watching for another opportunity of humiliating him, and would not be merciful in using it.

The change in her manner to him had been very sudden, as though she had on that particular day made up her mind about something concerning him. Hitherto she had treated him almost cordially, certainly with every appearance of liking him. He had even of late begun to fancy that her colour heightened when he entered the room, — a phenomenon which, if real, was attributable rather to another cause, and connected with Lawrence's presence in the house.

After dinner the whole party went out upon the verandah, a favourite manœuvre of Miss Cordelia's, whereby the society of Mr. Brinsley was not wasted upon smoke and men's talk in the dining-room. This evening, however, instead of sitting down at once in her usual place, Cordelia slipped her arm through Fanny's, and led her off to the other side and down the steps into the garden.

"The moonlight is so lovely," said Miss Cordelia, "and I want to talk to you. Let us walk a little — do you mind?"

The two went along the path in silence, in and out among the trees. The moon was full. From the sea came up the sound of the tide, washing the smooth rocks at high water. The breeze had died away at sunset and the deep sky was cloudless. Here and there the greater stars twinkled softly, but the little ones were all lost in the moonlight, like diamonds in a pure fountain. Everything was asleep except the watchful, wakeful sea. The two women stood still and looked across the lawn. At last Miss Miner spoke.

"Why were you so unkind to Mr. Brinsley to-night?" she asked in a low voice.

Fanny glanced at her before she answered. The eldest Miss Miner's face had once been almost beautiful. In the moonlight, the delicate, clearly chiselled features were lovely still, but a little ghostly, and the young girl saw that the fixed smile had disappeared for once, leaving a look of pain in its place.

"I didn't mean to be unkind," Fanny began.

"That is," she added quickly, correcting herself, "I'm not quite sure of what I meant. I think I did mean to hurt him. He's so strong, and he's always showing that he despises Mr. Lawrence, because he isn't an athlete. As though a man must be a prize-fighter to be nice!"

"Well — but — Mr. Lawrence doesn't mind.

You see how he takes it all. Why should you fight battles for him?"

"Perhaps I shouldn't. But — why should you take up the cudgels for Mr. Brinsley? He's quite able to take care of himself, if he will only tell the truth."

"If!" exclaimed Miss Cordelia, in ready resentment. "He's the most truthful man alive."

"Oh! And he told you he had been in the English navy."

"What has that to do with it? Of course he has, if he says so."

"He's unwise to say so, because he hasn't," answered Fanny, in her usual direct way.

"How in the world can you say that a man like Mr. Brinsley — an honourable man, I'm sure — is telling a deliberate falsehood? I'm surprised at you, Fanny — indeed I am! It isn't like you."

"Did you ever know me to tell you anything that wasn't exactly true?" asked the young girl, looking down into her elderly cousin's sweet, sad face, for she was much the taller.

"No — of course not — but —"

"Well, Cousin Cordelia, I tell you that your

Mr. Brinsley has never been in the English navy.
I don't say that I think so.   I say that I know it.
Will you believe me, or him?"

"Oh, Fanny!"   Miss Cordelia raised her eyes
with a frightened glance.

"Not that it matters," added Fanny, looking
away across the moonlit lawn again.   "Who
cares?   Only, it's one of those lies that go against
a man," she continued after a short pause.   "A
man may pretend that he has shot ten million
grisly bears in his back yard, or hooked a salmon
that weighed a hundred-weight — people will
laugh and say that he's a story-teller.   It's all
right, you know — and nobody minds.   But when
a man says he's been in the army or in the navy,
and hasn't — people call him a liar and cut him.
I don't know why it's so, I'm sure, but it is — and
we all know it."

"Yes," answered Cordelia, almost tremulously;
"but you haven't proved that Mr. Brinsley isn't
telling the truth — "

"Oh yes, I have!   There never was a deep-
sea sailor yet who had never heard of club-hauling a ship to save her.   I know about those

things.   I always make navy officers talk to me
about those things whenever I get a chance.
Besides, I can prove it to you.   Ask the first
captain of a fishing-schooner you meet down at
the landing what it means.   But don't tell me
I don't know — it's too absurd."

Miss Cordelia looked down.   Her hand still
rested on Fanny's arm, and it trembled now so
that the young girl felt it.

"What does it mean, then?" asked Cordelia,
faintly.

"Oh, it's a long operation to tell about.   It's
when you've got a lee-shore in a gale, and you
want to go about and can't, because you miss
stays every time, and you let go an anchor, and
the ship swings to it, and just as she begins to
get way on, you slip your chain, and she pays
off on the other tack.   Of course you lose your
anchor."

"Oh — you lose the anchor?   To save the
ship?   I see."

"Exactly."

"You lose the anchor to save the ship," repeated Cordelia, softly, as though she were try-

ing to remember the words for future use. Shall we go back?" she suggested, rather abruptly.

"I wish you'd answer me one question first," said Fanny.

"Yes. What is it?"

"Why are you so awfully anxious to stand up for Mr. Brinsley? You're not in love with him, are you?"

Cordelia started very perceptibly, and turned her face away. Then, all at once, she laughed a little hysterically.

"In love? At my age?"

And she laughed again, and laughed, strange to say, till she cried, clinging all the time to the young girl's strong arm. Fanny did not ask any more questions as they walked slowly back to the house.

CHAPTER VII.

"COME with me into the village, and help me to do errands," said Fanny on the following morning, just as Lawrence was feeling for his pipe in his pocket after breakfast. "You can smoke till we get there. It wouldn't hurt you to smoke less, anyway."

They went down through the garden, fresh and dewy still from the short, cool night, towards the sea. The path to the village lies along a low sea-wall, just high enough and strong enough to keep the tide from the lawns. But the tide was beginning to run out at that hour, and was singing and rocking itself away from the shore,

leaving the big loose stones and the chocolate-
coloured rocks all wet and shining in the morning sun. The breeze was springing up in the
offing and would reach the land before long, kiss-
ing each island as it passed softly by, and gently

breaking with dark blue the smoothly undulating
water.

The sun was almost behind the pair as they
walked along the sands, and shone full upon
the harbour as it came into view, lighting up
the deep green of the islands between which
passes the channel, and bringing up the warm
brown of the soil through thick weaving spruces.

The graceful yachts caught the sunshine, too, their hulls gleaming darkly, or dazzlingly white, their slender masts pencilled in light, against the trees, and standing out like threaded needles when they showed against the pale, clear sky. In the bright northern air, the artist would have complained that there was no atmosphere — no 'depth,' nor 'distance,' but only the distinct farness of the objects a long way off — nothing at all like 'atmospheric perspective.'

"Isn't it a glorious day!" exclaimed Fanny, looking seaward at a white-sailed fishing-schooner, which scarcely moved in the morning air.

"It's a little bit too swept and garnished," answered Lawrence. "That is — for a picture, you know. It's better to feel than to look at, if you understand what I mean. It feels so northern, that when you look at it, it seems bare and unfinished without a little snow."

"But you like it, don't you?" asked the young girl, in prompt protest.

"Of course I do. What a question! I thought I'd been showing how much I liked it, ever since I got here."

" I'm not sure that you show what you like and don't like," said Fanny, in a tone of reflexion. " Perhaps it's better not to."

" You don't, at all events. At least — aren't

you rather an inscrutable person? Of course I don't know," he added rather foolishly, pulling his woollen cap over his eyes and glancing at her sideways.

" Inscrutable! What a big word! ' The in-

I

scrutable ways of Providence ' — that's what they always say, don't they? Still — if you mean that I don't 'tell,' you're quite right. I don't — when I can keep my countenance. Do you? It's always far better not to tell. Besides, if you commit yourself to an opinion, you're committing yourself to gaol."

"What a way of putting it! But it's really true. I should so much like to ask you a question about one of your opinions."

"Why don't you?" asked Fanny, turning her eyes to his.

"Oh — lots of reasons: I'm afraid, in the first place; and then, I'm not sure you have one, and then —"

"Say it all — I hate people who hesitate!"

"Well — no. There's a great deal more to say than I want to say. Let's talk about the landscape."

"No. I want to know what the question is which you wished you might ask," insisted Fanny.

"It's about Mr. Brinsley," said Lawrence, plunging.

"Well, what about him?" Fanny's tone changed perceptibly, and her expression grew cold and forbidding.

"Nothing particular — unless it's impertinent — so I won't ask it."

"You won't?" asked Fanny, slackening her pace and looking hard at him. "Not if I ask you to?"

"No," answered Lawrence. "I'd oblige you by asking a different question, but not that one. You wouldn't know the difference."

"That's ingenuous, at all events." She looked away again and laughed.

"I never fight when I can help it, and you looked dangerous just now. You always are, in one way or another."

"What do you mean?"

"Only that when you don't happen to be frightening me out of my wits, you are charming me into a perfect idiot."

"Something between an express train and the Lorelei," laughed Fanny.

But the quick, girlish blood had sprung to her sunny cheeks and lingered a moment, as though it loved the light. They were now in the village

— in the broad street where the shops are. At that hour there were many people moving about on foot and in every sort of vehicle, short of brougham and landaus. There was the smart couple in a high buckboard, just out for a morning drive; there was the elderly farmer with his buggy or his hooded cart — his wife seated beside him, with her queer, sad, winter-blighted face, and her decent, but dusty black frock; — there was the young farmer 'sport' driving his favourite trotting horse in a sulky. And of pedestrians there was no end. A smart party bent on a day's excursion by sea came down the board walk, brilliant in perfectly new blue and white serge, with bits of splendid orange and red here and there, fresh faces, light hearts, great appetites, and the most trifling of cares — the care for trifles themselves. Fanny nodded and smiled, and was smiled at, while Lawrence attempted to lift his soft woollen cap from his head with some sort of grace — a thing impossible, as men who wear soft woollen caps well know. But the air seemed lighter and brighter for so much youth laughing in it.

Fanny dived into one shop after another, Lawrence following her, rather awkwardly, as a man always does under the circumstances, until he is old enough to find out that there is a time for watching as well as a time for talking, and that more may be learned of a woman's character from the way she treats shopkeepers than is generally supposed.   Fanny showed surprising alternations of firmness and condescension, for she had the gift of managing people and of getting what she wanted, which is a rare gift and one not to be despised.   She asked very kindly after the fishmonger's baby, but she did not hesitate to tell the grocer the hardest of truths about the butter.

"I always do my own marketing," she said to Lawrence, in answer to his look of surprise. "It amuses me, and I get much better things. My poor dear cousins don't understand marketing a bit — though they ought to.   That's the reason why they never get on, somehow.   I believe marketing is the best school in the world for learning what's worth having and what isn't. Don't you?"

"I never had a chance to learn," laughed Lawrence. "I wish you'd teach me how to get on, as you call it."

"Oh—it's very easy! You only need know exactly what you want, and then try to get it as hard as you can. Most people don't know, and don't try."

"For that matter I know perfectly well what I want."

"Then why don't you try and get it?" asked Fanny, pausing at the door of another shop as though interested in his answer.

"I'm not sure that it's in the market," answered the young man, his eyes in hers.

"Have you enquired?" Fanny's mouth twitched with the coming smile.

"No — not exactly. I'm trying to find out by inspection."

"If you don't think it's likely to be too dear, you'd better ask — whatever it is."

"Money couldn't buy it. Besides, I've got none," added Lawrence.

"You might get it on credit," said Fanny. "But I think it's very doubtful."

Thereupon she entered the shop, and Law-rence followed her, meditating deeply upon his chances, and asking himself whether he should run the great risk at once, or wait and watch Brinsley. To tell the truth, he thought his own chances very small; for he underestimated all his advantages by looking at them in the light of his present poverty, not seeing that in so doing he might be underestimating Fanny Trehearne as well. A somewhat excessive caution, which sometimes goes with timidity, though not at all of the sort which produces cowardice, is often the result of an education which has not brought a man closely into competition with other men. No one in common sense, save the Miss Miners and Lawrence himself, could have imagined that Brinsley had a chance against him. For any-thing that people knew, Brinsley might turn out to be an adventurer of the worst kind, whereas Lawrence was of good birth, a man of whom many knew who he was, and whence he came, and that he had as good a right to ask for Fanny's hand as any man. He was poor just now, but no one believed that his rich uncle, a childless widower of fifty-five, would marry again, and Lawrence was sure to have money in the end, though he might wait thirty years for it.

As for Brinsley, Fanny Trehearne either could not or would not pretend that she liked him, even in the most moderate degree of distant liking, after she had satisfied herself that he was not a truthful person in those matters in which truth decides the right of a man to be considered honourable. Being, on the whole, more careful than most people about the accuracy of what she said, she was less inclined to make allowances for others than a great many of her contemporaries. Besides, Brinsley had not only told a lie, which was mean in itself, but he had allowed himself to be found out, which Fanny considered contemptible.

Up to this time she had seemed to think him very pleasant company and not a bad addition to the society of the place.

" He's so good-looking!" she had often said to the approving Miss Miners. " And he has good manners, and knows how to come into a room, and how to sit down and get up — and do lots of things," she added vaguely.

In this opinion her three old-maid cousins fully concurred, and they were quite ready to say as much in his favour as Fanny could have heard without laughing. They were therefore greatly distressed when she changed her mind.

" He's handsome," Fanny now admitted. " But he's a little too showy. I've seen men like him at races, but they were not the men who were introduced to me. I don't think they knew anybody I knew — that sort of man, don't you know? And his English accent isn't quite English, and I don't like his little flat whiskers, and his hands irritate me. Besides, he said he had been in the navy, and now he admits that he never was. That's enough."

" My dear Fanny," Cordelia answered, on such occasions, " there was a misunderstanding about that, you know. He was in the navy, since he was an officer of Marines, but of course he wasn't expected to know — "

" The Marines!" exclaimed Fanny, contempt-

uously. " It's only a way of getting out of it,
I'm sure ! "

Thereupon the three Miss Miners told her
that she was very unjust and prejudiced, as they
retired together to praise Mr. Brinsley, out of
hearing of their young cousin's tart comment.
Miss Cordelia had made it all right by giving the
man an opportunity of justifying himself after he
had privately explained to her that the Marines
were an integral part of the navy, but that they
were not called upon to know anything about
navigation, — a fact which must account for his
ignorance.

He had very firm friends, to say the least of it,
in the three spinsters, who might have been said
to worship the ground on which he walked, and
who thought it a sin and a shame that Fanny
should treat him as she did.   As for young Lawrence, he looked on, with his observant artist's
eyes, and never mentioned Brinsley, except to
Fanny herself.   For he was not at all lacking in
tact, however deficient he might be in the manly
accomplishments.

" Do you know," Fanny began, one day when

Duck Brook.

they were walking in the woods, " I don't half mind your being such a bad hand at things. It's funny. I thought I should, at first — but I don't."

" I'm awfully glad," answered Lawrence, not finding anything else to say to express his gratitude.

" Oh, you may well be ! " laughed Fanny. " I don't forgive everybody for being a duffer. And that's what you are, you know. You don't mind my saying so ? "

" Oh no, not at all." The tone in which he spoke did not express much conviction, however.

" I believe you do," said Fanny, thoughtfully.

They were following a narrow path which led upwards along the bank of a brook under over-arching trees. Here and there the bank had fallen away, and the woodmen had laid down 'slabs' of the rippings first taken off by the saw-mill in squaring timber. It was damp under foot, for it had lately rained, and the wet, choco-late-coloured dead leaves of the previous year filled the chinks between the bits of wood, and sometimes lay all over them, a slippery mass. It was still and hot and damp all through the thick growth on the midsummer's afternoon. The whispered mystery of countless living things filled the quiet air with a vibration more felt than heard, which overcame the silence, but did not break the stillness.

The path was very narrow, and Fanny had to walk before her companion. Their voices seemed to echo back to them from very near, as they talked, for amongst the trees the rich under-growth grew man-high. On their right, below them, the brook laughed softly to itself as a faun might laugh, drowsily, half asleep in a hollow of the deep woods.

And then, through the warm-breathing secret places, where all that was living was growing fiercely in the sudden summer, stole the heart-thrilling fragrance of all that lived, than which nothing more surely stirs young blood in the glory of the year.

For some minutes the pair walked on in silence, Fanny leading. The young man watched the strong, lithe figure of the girl as she moved swiftly and sure-footed before him. Suddenly she stopped, without turning round, and she seemed to be listening. A low ray of sunlight ran quivering through the trees and played with a crisp ringlet of her hair, too full of life and strength to be smoothed to dull order with the rest.

" What is it ? " asked Lawrence, in a low voice, watching her.

" I thought I heard some one in the woods," she answered quickly, and then listened again.

Not a sound broke the dream-like stillness.

" I'm sure I heard something," said Fanny. Then she laughed a little. " Besides," she added, " it's very likely. It's awfully hot. " Here's a good place to sit down."

It was not a particularly good place, being damp and sloping, and Lawrence planted his heels firmly amongst the wet, dead leaves to keep himself from slipping down into the path as he sat beside her.

" There's always something going on in the woods," she said softly and dreamily. " The trees talk to each other all day long, and the squirrels sit and crack nuts while they listen to the conversation. I like the woods. Somehow one never feels alone when one gets where things grow — does one?"

"I don't mind being alone when I can't be — I mean — " Lawrence did not finish his sentence, but bent down and picked up a twig from the ground. "Isn't it funny!" he exclaimed, twisting it in his hands. "All the bark's loose, and turns round."

"Of course — it's an old twig, and it's wet. When don't you mind being alone? You were saying something — 'when you couldn't be with' — something, or somebody."

"Oh — you know! What's the use of my saying it?" Lawrence kept his eye on the twig.

"I don't know, and if I want you to say anything, that's the use," answered Fanny, whose prose style, so to say, was direct if it was anything.

"Yes — but you see — I didn't mean anything in particular." He broke the twig in two and tossed it over the path into the brook below.

Fanny changed her position a little, leaning forward and clasping her gloved hands round her knees.

Duck Brook.

K

" You're very nice, you know," she said meditatively. " I like you."

" Because I don't answer your questions? "
asked Lawrence, looking at her face, which was
half turned from him.

" Yes. That's one of the reasons."

" It's a very funny one. I don't see much reason
in it, I confess."

" Don't you? Don't you know that a woman
sometimes likes a man for what he doesn't
say? "

" I never thought of it in that way. I daresay
you're right. You ought to know much better
than I do. Especially if you really like me, as
you say you do."

" Oh — I'm honest. I never said I'd been in
the navy!" Fanny laughed. " Besides, if I
didn't like you, why should I say so? Just to
say something civil? The way Mr. Brinsley
does? "

" Brinsley's a horror! Don't talk about him
— especially here."

" I don't mean to. I hate him. But if we
were going to talk about him, this would be a

good place — one's sure that he's not just round
the corner of the verandah making one of my
three cousins miserable."

"How do you mean?"

"Why — they all love him. Can't you see
it? I don't mean figuratively. Not a bit.
They're in love with him, poor dears!"

"Nonsense! not really?" Lawrence laughed
incredulously.

"Yes — really. It's a rather dismal sort of
love — they've kept their hearts in pickle for
such an age, you know — old pickles aren't good,
either. I've no patience with old maids who
fall in love and make fools of themselves!"

"Perhaps they can't help it," suggested the
young man. "Nobody can help falling in love,
you know."

"No," answered Fanny, rather doubtfully.
"Perhaps not. I don't know. It depends."

"People don't generally try to keep themselves from falling in love," remarked Lawrence,
with the air of a philosopher. "It's more apt
to be the other way. They are generally trying
to make some one else fall in love with them.
That's the hard thing."

" Is it ? " Fanny smiled. " Perhaps it is," she added, after a pause. " I'd like to tell you something — "

She hesitated and stopped. Lawrence looked at her, but did not speak, expecting her to go on. The silence continued for some time. Once or twice Fanny turned and met his eyes, and her lips moved as though she were just going to say something. She seemed to be in doubt.

" I don't believe in friendship, and I don't believe in promises, — and I don't believe much in anything," she said, at last, in magnificent generalization. " But I'd like to tell you, all the same. Do you mind ? "

" I won't repeat it if you do," said Lawrence, simply.

" No — I don't believe you will. You see I haven't any friends, so I never tell things, — at least, not much. I don't believe much in telling, anyway. Do you ? "

" Not if you mean to keep a secret."

" Oh — well — this isn't exactly a secret — only I don't want any one to know it. Yes, I know! You laugh because I'm going to tell you. But you're different, somehow — "

"Am I?"

"Oh yes, — you don't count!"

Lawrence's face fell a little at this last remark, and there was silence again for a few moments.

"I'm not sure that I'll tell you, after all," said Fanny, at last.

The quiet lids were half closed over the grey eyes, and she seemed to be thinking out something. Lawrence was unconsciously wondering why he did not think the white lashes ugly, especially when she had just told him that he did not 'count.'

"Are you sure you won't tell?" asked the young girl, after another long pause.

"If you don't want me to, of course I won't," answered Lawrence, mechanically.

"It's a sort of confession," said Fanny. "That's the reason why I don't like to tell you. It's cowardly to be afraid of confessing that one's been an idiot, so I am going to do it at once and get it over."

"It's a startling confession!" laughed Lawrence, softly. "I don't believe it. Is that all?"

In the Woods.

" If you laugh at me, I won't tell you anything more. Then you'll be sorry."

" Shall I ? "

" Yes."

" All right ! I'm serious now," said Lawrence.

" Don't you want to smoke ? " asked Fanny, suddenly. " I wish you would. I should be less — less nervous, you know."

" What a curious idea ! But I'll smoke if you like."

He proceeded to fill and light a big brier-root pipe.

" I like the smell of a pipe," said Fanny, watching the operation. " I'm so tired of the everlasting cigarette."

" I'm ready," Lawrence said, puffing slowly into the still, hot air.

" Are you sure you won't laugh at me ? Well, I'll tell you. I liked Mr. Brinsley awfully — at first."

Lawrence looked at her quickly and took his pipe from his mouth.

" Not really ? " he exclaimed, only half-interrogatively, but with a change of colour. " But

then — well — I don't suppose you mean anything particular by that," he added, to comfort
himself. "You don't mean that you —" He
stopped.

Fanny nodded slowly, and the blush that rose
in her face reddened her sunny complexion.

"Yes.   That's what I mean.   I cared for him,
you know, — that sort of thing."

"It hasn't taken you long to get over it, at
all events," answered Lawrence, gravely, and
wondering inwardly why she made the extraordinary confession, seeing that it hurt him and
could do her no good.

"No — it hasn't taken long, has it?   That's
what frightens me.   If I weren't frightened, I
shouldn't talk to you about it."

"I don't understand — why are you frightened?
Especially since you've got over it.   I don't
see —"

"I thought you might," said Fanny, enigmati-
cally.

A long silence followed, this time.   Lawrence
crossed his hands on his knees as Fanny was
doing, holding his pipe, which was going out.

Duck Brook.

They both sat staring at the opposite bank of the brook.

The vital loveliness of the still woods was all around them, whispering in their young ears, breathing into their young nostrils the breath of nature's life, caressing them with bountiful warmth. They sat side by side, very near, staring at the opposite bank, and for a long time no words passed their lips. At last the young girl spoke in a low and almost monotonous tone.

" He has an influence over people who come near him," she said. " Besides, that kind of man appeals to me. It's natural, isn't it? I'm so fond of all sorts of things out-of-doors, that I can't help admiring a man who can do everything so well. And he's a splendid creature. You've never seen him ride. You don't know — it's wonderful! I wish you could see him on that thoroughbred Teddy Van De Water has brought up this summer — Teddy's a good rider, but he can't do anything with the mare. You ought to see Brinsley — Mr. Brinsley — you'd understand better."

" But I understand perfectly, as it is," said Lawrence, rather gloomily.

" Do you? I wonder whether you really do. Do you think there's any — any excuse for me ? "

The words were spoken in a faltering shame-faced way very unlike Fanny's usual manner.

" As though you needed any excuse for taking a fancy to any one who pleases you ! " answered Lawrence, rather coldly. " Aren't you perfectly free to like anybody who turns up ? "

During the pause which followed, he slowly relighted his pipe, which had quite gone out by this time.

" I was afraid you wouldn't understand," said Fanny, in a disappointed tone.

" But I do — "

" No — not what I mean. I hate explaining things, but I shall have to."

Louis Lawrence wondered vaguely what there could be to explain, and, if there were anything, why she should be so anxious to explain to him in particular.

CHAPTER VIII.

I T was in this way," said Fanny. " Mr. Brinsley brought a letter of introduction from Cousin Frank. You know who Frank is, don't you? He's the brother of the three Miss Miners."

" Of course," nodded Lawrence. " Everybody knows Frank Miner."

" And he knows everybody. But he didn't say much in his note, and Cordelia has written to him since, because she wants to know all about Mr. Brinsley, and it appears that Frank has only met him once or twice at a club, and doesn't know anything about him. However, it doesn't matter! The main point is that he called the

day after we got here, and in twenty-four hours
we were all in love with him."

"Please don't include yourself," said Lawrence,
his delicate face betraying that he winced.

"I will include myself, because it's true,"
answered Fanny, very much in earnest. "I
shouldn't put it just in that way about myself,
perhaps, — but I took a fancy to him, and I took
him to drive, and I found that he could drive
quite as well as I, and we went out riding
with a party, and he rides like an angel — he
really does — it's divine. And then I tried him
in the boat, and he was good at that. So I began to like him very much."

"They're all excellent reasons for liking a
man," observed Lawrence, with a little contempt.

"Don't scoff at things you can't do yourself,"
said Fanny, severely. "It's not in good taste.
Besides, I don't care. All women admire men
who are stronger, and quicker, and better with
their hands than other men. One always thinks
they must be braver, too."

"Yes, that's true," assented Lawrence, seeking
to retrieve himself by meekness.

" And they generally are. It takes courage to ride well, and it needs nerve to handle a boat in a squall. I don't mean to say that you can't be brave if you don't know how to do those things. That would be nonsense. You — for instance — you could learn. Only nobody has ever taught you anything, and you're getting old."

Lawrence laughed outright, and forgot his ill-humour in a moment.

" Oh — I don't mean really old," said Fanny, immediately. " I only mean that one ought to learn when one is a child, as I did. Then it's no trouble, you see — and one never forgets. Now, Mr. Brinsley began young — "

" Yes," interrupted the young man, " I should say so. I'm sorry I didn't."

" So am I. It would have been so nice to do things — "

She stopped abruptly, and pulled up a blade of rank grass, which she proceeded to twist thoughtfully round her finger.

" I shouldn't like you to think I was a flirt," she said, suddenly turning her grey eyes upon him.

L

He met her glance curiously, being considerably surprised by her remark.

" Because I sometimes think I am, myself," she added, still looking at him. " Do you think so? " she asked earnestly. " What is a flirt, anyway? "

" A woman who draws a man on for the pleasure of breaking his heart, I suppose," answered Lawrence, keeping his eyes fixed intently on hers.

" Then I'm only half a flirt," said Fanny, " because I only draw a man on, without meaning to break anybody's heart."

" Don't," said Lawrence. - " It hurts, you know."

" I wonder — " The young girl laughed a little, and turned away from his eyes.

" What ? "

" Whether it really hurts." She bit the end of the grass blade, and slowly tore it with her teeth, looking dreamily across the brook.

" Don't try it, at all events."

" Mr. Brinsley doesn't seem to mind."

" Brinsley isn't a human being," said Lawrence, savagely.

" What is he, then ? "

" A fraud — of some sort. 'I don't care. I hate him ! "

" You're hard on Mr. Brinsley," observed Fanny, slowly, and watching her companion sideways.

" Considering what you've been saying about him — "

" I said nothing about him except that I began by liking him awfully."

" Well — you left the rest to my imagination. I did as well as I could. If you didn't hate him yourself, you'd hardly have been telling me all this, would you ? "

" Oh — I don't know. I might be going to ask your advice about — about him."

" Take him out in your boat and drown him," suggested Lawrence. " That's my advice about him."

" What has he done to you, Mr. Lawrence ? " enquired Fanny, gravely. " Why do you hate him so ? "

" Why ? It's plain enough, it seems to me — plain as a — what do you call the thing ? "

" Plain as a marlinespike, you mean. Only it isn't. I want to know two things. Do you think I'm a flirt? And why do you want me to murder poor, innocent Mr. Brinsley? Do you mind answering? "

Lawrence's dark eyes began to gleam angrily. He bit his pipe and pulled at it, though it had gone out; then he took it from his lips and answered deliberately.

" If you are a flirt, Miss Trehearne, I don't wish Brinsley any further damage. He'll do very well in your hands, I'm sure. I have no anxiety."

" I wouldn't hurt a fly," said Fanny. " If I liked the fly," she added.

" I believe the spider said something to the same effect, when he invited the fly into his parlour."

At this a dark flush rose in the girl's cheeks.

" You're rude, Mr. Lawrence," she said.

" I'm sorry, Miss Trehearne — but you're un-kind, so you'll please to excuse me."

Instead of flushing, as she did, Lawrence turned slowly pale, as was his nature.

" Even if I were, — but I'm not, — that's no reason why you should be rude."

" I didn't mean to be rude," answered Lawrence. " I don't see what I said that was so very dreadful."

" It was much worse than anything I said," retorted Fanny, biting her blade of grass again. " Because I didn't say anything at all, you know. Oh, well — if you'll say you're sorry, we'll bury it."

" I'm sorry," said Lawrence, without the least show of contrition.

" I was going to tell you such lots of things about myself," said the young girl. " You've made me forget them all. What was I talking about when we began to fight? I began by saying that I liked you, and you've been horrid ever since. I won't say that again, at all events."

" Excuse me — you began by saying that you'd liked Brinsley — liked him awfully, you said. It must have been awful — anything connected with Brinsley is necessarily awful."

" There you go again. Don't bolt so — it

makes bad running. I told you why I liked him so much at first, and you admitted that it was natural. Do you remember that? Well — that isn't all. After I liked him, I began to care for him. I told you that, too. Horrid of me, wasn't it?"

"Horrid!"

"I wish you wouldn't agree with me all the time!" exclaimed Fanny, impatiently. "You know I really did care — a little. And then one day in the catboat, he asked me —" She stopped and looked at Lawrence.

"To marry you? Why don't you say it? It wouldn't surprise me a bit."

"No," said Fanny, slowly, "he didn't ask me to marry him."

"In Heaven's name, what did he ask you?" enquired Lawrence, exasperated to impatience.

"Oh — I don't know. It was something about the channel between Bar and Sheep, I believe. Nothing very important, anyway. I'm not sure that I could remember, if I tried."

"Then, — excuse me, but what's the point?"

"Oh — I know!" exclaimed Fanny, as though

suddenly recollecting something. " Not that it matters much, but I like to be accurate. It was about the bell buoy off Sheep Porcupine. You know, I showed it to you the other day. Well — I told him how it had been carried away in a storm some time ago, and that this was a new one. And the next day I heard him telling Augusta all about it, as though he had known before, you see."

" Well — that wasn't exactly a crime," observed Lawrence, who could not understand at all. " You'd told him — "

" Yes, but he said he remembered the old one. That was impossible, as he hadn't known anything about it. It was a little slip, but it made me open my eyes and watch him. I used to think he was perfection until then."

" Oh, I see ! That was when you first began to find out that he wasn't quite straight."

" Exactly. It made all the difference. I've caught him out more than once since then. The other night, it was too much for me when he talked about the navy — so I promptly smashed him. He knows that I know, now."

"I should think so. All the same — I don't
mean to be rude this time, Miss Trehearne — "

"Be careful!"

"No — I'll risk it. Just now when you said
he had 'asked you' — you stopped short. You
knew I should believe that you had been going
to say that he had asked you to marry him,
didn't you?"

"Oh, I know! I couldn't help it — I believe
I really am a flirt, after all."

"I shouldn't like to believe it," said Lawrence,
gravely.

"Nor I — either. I only wanted to see how
you'd look if you thought he'd offered himself
just then."

"Just then! Do you mean to say that he has
offered himself at any other time?"

"Now you're rude again — only, I forgive you,
because you don't know that you are. It's rude
to ask such questions — so I'll be polite and
refuse to answer. Not that there's any good
reason why he shouldn't have asked me to marry
him, you know. The fact that you hate him
isn't a reason."

"But you do, yourself — "

"Not at all. At least, I haven't said so. I wish you'd listen to me, Mr. Lawrence, instead of interrupting me with questions every other moment. How in the world am I to make a confession, if you won't let me say two words?"

"Are you going to make a confession?" asked Lawrence, incredulously. "It's all chaff, you know!"

Fanny turned her cool eyes upon him instantly.

"There's a lot besides chaff," she said, in a very different tone. "I can be in earnest, too — when I care."

She certainly emphasized the last three words in a way which might have meant much, accompanied as they were by her steady look. Lawrence felt himself growing a little pale again.

"Do you care?" he asked, and his voice shook perceptibly.

"For Mr. Brinsley?" enquired Fanny, instantly changing her tone again and beginning to laugh.

"No — for me."

" For you!   Oh dear, what a question!"   She laughed outright.

Lawrence leaned down and knocked the ashes out of his pipe against the toe of his heavy walking-shoe without saying a word.   Then he put the pipe into his pocket.   She watched him.

" You've no right to be angry this time," she said.   " But you are."

The young man faced her quietly and waited a moment before he spoke.

" You're playing with me," he said, calmly and without emphasis, as stating a fact.

" Of course I am!" laughed Fanny Trehearne. " What did you expect?   But I'm sorry that you've found it out," she added, with appalling cynicism.   " It won't be fun any more."

" Unless we both play," suggested Lawrence, who had either recovered his temper very quickly, or possessed a better control over it than Fanny had supposed.

" All right!" she exclaimed cheerfully.   " Let's play — let us play.   That sounds solemn, some-how — I wonder why?   Oh — of course — it's like ' Let us pray ' in church."

Lawrence laughed drily.

" Let us pray beforehand, for the one who gets the worst of it," he said. " He or she will need it. But I shall win at the game, you know. That's a foregone conclusion."

Fanny was surprised and amused at the confidence he suddenly affected — very unlike his habitual modesty and self-effacement.

" You seem pretty sure of .yourself," she answered. " What shall the forfeit be, as they say in the children's games ? "

" To marry or not to marry, at the discretion of the winner. I think that's fair, don't you? I shouldn't like to propose anything serious — the head of Roger Brinsley in a charger, for instance."

Fanny laughed again.

" Yes, it's all very well ! " she protested. " But of course the one who loses will be in earnest, and the one who wins will not."

" He may be, by that time," suggested Lawrence.

" Don't say 'he,' so confidently — I mean to win. Besides, are we starting fair ? Of course

I don't care an atom for you, but don't you care for me — just a little? "

" I ! " exclaimed Lawrence. " What an idea ! " He laughed quite as naturally as Fanny herself. " Do you think that a man in love would propose such a game as we are talking about ? " he asked.

" I'm sure I don't know what to think," answered the young girl. " Perhaps I shall know in a day or two."

She looked down, quite grave again, and pulled a bit of fern from the bank, and crushed it in her hand, and then smelled it.

" Don't you like sweet fern ? " she asked, holding it out to him. " I love it ! "

" That's why you crush it, I suppose," said Lawrence.

" It doesn't smell sweet unless you do. Oh — I see ! You were beginning to play the game. Very well. Why should we lose time about it ? But I wish it were a little better defined. What is it we're going to do ? Won't you explain ? I'm so stupid about these things. Are we going to flirt for a bet ? "

" What a speech !"

" Because it's a plain one ? Is that why you object to it ? After all, that's what we said."

" We only said we'd play," answered Lawrence. " Whichever ends by caring must agree to marry the winner, if required. But I'm afraid the time is too short," he added, more gravely. " I've only a week more."

" Only a week !" exclaimed Fanny, in a tone of disappointment. " Why, I thought there was ever so much more. That isn't nearly time enough."

" We must play faster — and hope for ' situations,' as they call them on the stage."

" Oh — the situation is bad enough, as it is," answered the young girl, with a change of manner that surprised her companion. " If you only knew !"

" Was that what you were going to tell me about ?" asked Lawrence, quickly, and with renewed interest. " I thought you were making game of me."

" That's the trouble ! You'll never believe

that I'm in earnest, now. That's the worst of
practical jokes. Come along! We must be
going home. The sun's behind the hill and ever
so low, I'm sure. We shan't get home before

dusk. How sweet that fern smells! Give it
back to me, won't you?"

They rose and began to walk homeward in the
warm shadow of the woods. As before, Fanny
went first along the narrow path, and Lawrence,
following close behind her, and watching the

supple grace of her as she moved, breathed in also the intoxicating perfume of the aromatic sweet fern which she still carried in her hand.

CHAPTER IX.

O N the following afternoon Fanny Trehearne announced her intention of
riding with Mr. Brinsley.

"I'd take you, too," she said to
Lawrence, with a singularly cold stare. "Only
as you can't ride much, you wouldn't enjoy it,
you know."

"Certainly not," answered Lawrence, returning
her glance with all coolness. "I shouldn't enjoy
it at all."

"You might take my cousins out in the boat,
instead."

"Are they tired of life?" enquired the young
man, smiling. "No. I want to make a sketch
in the woods. I'll go out by myself, thank you."

"Do you mean to sketch the place where we stopped yesterday?"

"Oh no — I'm going in quite another direction. I can't exactly explain where it is, because I've such a bad memory for names of roads, and all that. But I can find it."

Miss Cordelia Miner looked up from the magazine she was reading.

"You're not going to ride alone with Mr. Brinsley, are you?" she asked suddenly.

"Why not?" asked Fanny. "I don't see any reason why I shouldn't. It's safer than riding alone, isn't it?"

"I confess, I don't like the idea," said Miss Cordelia. "It looks as though there were something."

"Something of what kind?" Fanny watched Lawrence's face.

"Something — well — not really an engagement — but —"

"Well — why shouldn't I be engaged to Mr. Brinsley, if I like?" enquired the young girl, arching her brows.

"Why, Fanny! I'm surprised!" And, indeed,

M

Miss Miner seemed so, for she almost sprang out of her chair.

"I don't know why you need be horrified, though," returned Fanny, calmly. "Should you be shocked if any one said that you were engaged to Mr. Brinsley? What's the matter with him, anyway?" she demanded, dropping into her favourite slang. "You'd be proud to be engaged to him — so would Elizabeth — so would Augusta! Then why shouldn't I be proud if I can get him? I'm sure, he's awfully good-looking, and he rides — like an angel."

"An angel jockey," suggested Lawrence, without a smile.

"Not at all!" exclaimed Fanny. "He rides like a gentleman and not in the least like a jockey."

Miss Cordelia had risen from her chair, and turned her back on the young people.

"You've no right to say such things to me, Fanny," she said, going slowly towards the window. Her voice shook.

The young girl saw that she was deeply hurt, and followed her quickly.

"I didn't mean to be horrid!" said Fanny, penitently. "I was only laughing, you know, and of course I shall take Stebbins. And I'm not engaged to Mr. Brinsley at all."

"Why didn't you say so at once?" asked Cordelia, half choking, and turning away her face.

Fanny, unseen by her cousin, glanced at Lawrence, and then at the door, and the young man departed immediately, leaving the two cousins to make peace.

He did not remain long in the house. Thrusting a sketch-book and a pencil into his pocket, with his pipe and pouch, he went out without seeing Fanny again, taking her at her word with regard to her plans for the afternoon. An hour later, he was seated under a tree high upon the side of the hill and almost out of sight of the Otter Cliff road. There was nothing particular in the way of a view from that point, but there were endless trees, and Lawrence amused himself in making a rough study of a mixed group of white pines, firs, and hackmatacks.

He did not draw very carefully, nor even industriously, and more than once he stopped working altogether for a quarter of an hour at a time. His principal object in coming had been to get out of the way just a little more promptly and completely than Fanny could have expected. His thoughts were much more concerned with her than with what he was doing.

Naturally enough, he was trying to understand the real bent of the girl's feelings. Setting aside the absurd chaff which had formed a good deal of the conversation on the previous afternoon, he tried to extract from it enough of truth to guide him, aiding himself by recalling little circumstances as well as words, for the one had often belied the other.

He saw clearly that Fanny Trehearne might have said to him, 'I like you, but I do not love you — win me if you can!' But it was like her to propose to 'flirt for a bet'—being at heart perhaps less of a flirt than she laughingly admitted herself to be. But that was not the point which chiefly interested him. What he wished to know was, just how far that undefined liking for him extended. To speak in the common phrase, he did not 'know where he was' with her, and it seemed that he had no means of finding out. On the other hand, he knew very well indeed that he himself was badly in love. The symptoms were not to be mistaken, nor had he been in love so often already as to make him sceptical as to what he felt. He was more distrustful of the result than of the impulse.

In his opinion Fanny was much too frank to be a flirt. Her directness was one of her principal charms, though he could not help suspecting that it must be one of her chief weapons. A little hesitation is often less deceptive than clear-eyed, outspoken truth. But Lawrence was no more able than most men of his age — or, indeed, of any age — to follow out a continuous train of thought where a woman was concerned. It is more often the woman's personality that concerns us, unreasoning men, than the probable direction of her own reasoning about us. We do not make love to an argument, so to speak, nor to a set of ideas, nor to a preconceived opinion of our merits or demerits. We make love to our own idea of what the woman is — and the depth of our disillusionment is the measure of our sincerity, when love is gasping between the death-blow and the death.

Moreover, what is called nowadays analysis of human nature, belongs in reality to transcendental thought. 'Transcendent' is defined as designating that which lies beyond the bounds of all possible experience. So far as we know, it is beyond those bounds to enter into the intelligence of our neighbour, subjectively, to identify ourselves with him and to see and understand the world with his eyes and mind. It follows that we are never sure of what we are doing when we attempt to set down exactly another man's train of thought, and it follows also that few are willing to recognize the result as at all resembling the process of which they are conscious within themselves. On certain bases, all men can appeal subjectively to all men, and all women to all women. But, as between the sexes, all observation is objective and tentative, whether it be that of the author, condemned to analyze a woman's character, or that of the man in love and attempting to understand the woman he loves.

And further, if we could see — as it is pretended by some that we can see on paper — precisely what is taking place in the intelligence of those we meet in the world, our friends would be as unrecognizable to us as a dissected man is unrecognizable for a human being except in the eyes of a doctor. The soul, laid bare, dissected, and turned inside out, with real success, would not be recognized by its dearest friend, were it ever so truthful a soul. We are all fundamentally and totally incapable of expressing exactly what we feel, and as we have no means of conveying truth without some sort of expression, we are helpless and are all more or less hopelessly misunderstood — a fact to which, if we please, we may ascribe that variety which is proverbially said to be the charm of life. Doubtless, this is a literary heresy; but it is a human truth a little above literature.

Lawrence had never attempted to write a book, but as he sat on the slope above the Otter

Cliff road, drawing trees, it did not occur to him to draw a picture of what he thought about the inside of each tree, instead of a representation of what he saw. But he made the usual fruitless attempt to understand the woman he loved, and to reason about her, and failed to do either, which is also usual. The conclusion he reached was that he loved her, of which he had been aware before he had set himself to think it out.

What he saw was a strong girl's face with cool, inscrutable grey eyes that never took fire and gleamed, nor ever turned dull and vacant. Their unchanging steadiness contradicted the wayward speech, the sudden capricious confidence, even the gay laugh, sometimes. Lawrence had a lively impression that whatever Fanny said or did, she never meant but one thing, whatever that might be. And with this impression he was obliged to content himself.

From the place where he sat, he had a glimpse between the trees of the road below. On the side towards him there was a little open bit of meadow, where the gorge widened, and a low fence with a little ditch separated it from the highway. On the hillside, above this stretch of grass, the trees grew here and there, wide apart at first, and then by degrees more close together. He himself was seated just within the thick wood, at the edge of the first underbrush.

Now and then, people passed along the road: a light buckboard drawn by a pair of bays and containing a smart-looking couple, with no groom behind; a farmer's wagon, long, hooded, and dusty, dragged at a disjointed trot by a broken-down grey horse; a solitary rider, whose varnished shoes reflected the sunlight even to where Lawrence was sitting; a couple of pedestrians; a lad driving a cow; and then another buckboard; and so on.

Lawrence was thinking of shutting up his book and climbing higher up the steep side of Newport Mountain — as the hill is called — in search of another study, when, glancing down through the trees, he saw three riders coming slowly along the road — two in front, and one at some distance behind — a lady and gentleman and then a groom. His eyes were good, and he would have known

Fanny Trehearne's figure and bearing even at a
greater distance. She sat so straight — hands
down, elbows in, head high, square in her saddle
yet flexible, and all moving with every movement
of her Kentucky thoroughbred. They came
nearer, and Lawrence saw them distinctly now.
Brinsley was beside her. Lawrence laughed to
himself at the idea that the man could ever have
been in the Marines. He sat the horse he rode
much more like a Mexican or an Indian than like
a sailor or a marine. Even at that distance Lawrence could not help admiring his really magnificent figure, for Brinsley's perfections were showy
and massed well afar off.

The riders reached the point where the little
meadow spread out on their left, and to Lawrence's surprise, they halted and seemed to be
consulting about something. They had turned
towards him, and as they talked, he could see
that Fanny looked across the meadow and up at
the woods where he was sitting. It was of course
utterly impossible that she should have known
where he was, and it was almost incredible that
she should see him, seated low upon the ground

On the Mountain.

in the deep shade, when she was only visible to him between the stems of the trees. Nevertheless, not caring to be discovered, he crouched down amongst the ferns and grasses, still keeping his eye on the couple in the road far below.

Presently he saw Fanny turn her horse's head, walk her to the other side of the road, and turn again, facing the meadow. She looked up and down the road once, saw that no one was coming, and put her mare at the fence. It was a low one, and the ditch on the outer side was neither broad nor deep. The thoroughbred cleared it with a contemptuously insignificant effort, and cantered a few strides forward into the grass, shaking her bony head almost between her knees as Fanny brought her to a stand and turned again. Brinsley followed her on the big Hungarian horse he rode, — Mr. Trehearne's horse, — jumping the fence and ditch, and taking them again almost immediately, to wait for Fanny on the other side in the road. She followed again, and pulled up by his side. But they did not ride on at once. They seemed to be discussing some point connected with the place, for they pointed here and there with their hands as they spoke. Fanny reined in her mare and backed a little, as though she were going to jump again. The animal seemed nervous, stamping and pawing, and laying back her small ears.

A hundred yards or more in the direction from which they had come the road made a short bend round the foot of the spur of the hill, known as Pickett's. Just as Fanny put the mare at the fence a third time, a coach and four turned the corner of the road at a smart pace, leaders cantering and wheelers at a long trot.

Seeing three horses apparently halting in the way, some one in the coach sent a terrific and discordant blast from a post-horn ringing along the road as a warning. At that moment Fanny's mare was rising at the bars. She cleared them as easily as ever, but on reaching the ground instantly bolted across the grass, head down, ears back, heels flying. It all happened in a moment. The two men, Brinsley and groom, knew too much to scare the thoroughbred by a pursuit, and confident in Fanny's good riding, sat motionless on their horses in the road, after drawing away enough to let the coach pass.

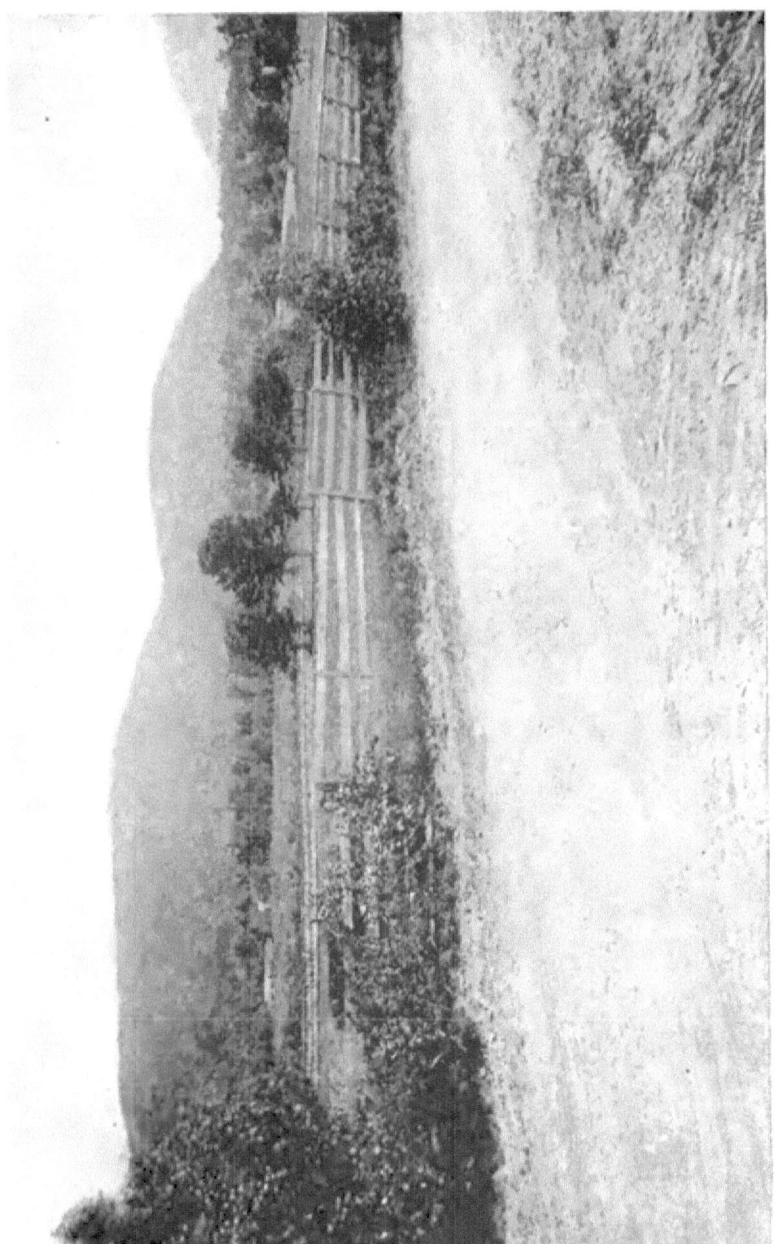

Meadow on Otter Cliff Road.

The idiot with the horn continued to blow fiercely, and the big vehicle came swinging along at a great rate, with clattering of hoofs, for the road was hard and dry-baked after a recent rain — and with jingling of harness and sound of voices. The mare grew more and more frightened, and tore up the hillside like a flash, directly away from the noise. The young girl was a first-rate rider and knew the fearful danger, if she should be carried at such a pace amongst the trees. But her strength, great as it was, for a woman, was not able to produce the slightest impression upon the terrified creature she rode.

Lawrence knew nothing of riding, but the imminent peril of the woman he loved was clear to him in a moment. He had a horrible vision of the wild-eyed mare tearing straight towards him through the trees — wide apart at first, and then dangerously near together.

On they came, the thoroughbred swerving violently at one stem after another — the young girl's strong figure swaying to her balance at each headlong movement. He could see her set

N

face, pale under the tan, and he could see the
desperate exertion of her strength.   He sprang
forward and ran down between the trees at the
top of his speed.

CHAPTER X.

THERE is nothing equal to the absolute fearlessness of a naturally brave man who has no experience of the risk he runs and is bent on saving the life of the woman he loves. Louis Lawrence remembered afterwards what he had done and how he had done it, but he was unconscious of what he was doing at the time.

He rushed down the hill between the closer trees, and with utter recklessness sprang at the bridle as the infuriated mare dashed past him. Grasping snaffle and curb — tight drawn as they were — in both hands, he threw all his light weight upon them and allowed himself to be

dragged along the ground between the trees at
the imminent risk of his life — a risk so terrible
that Fanny Trehearne turned paler for him than
for her own danger. In half a dozen more
strides they might both have been killed. But
the mare stopped, quivering, tried to rear, but
could not lift Lawrence far from the ground nor
shake off his desperate hold, plunged once and
again, and then stood quite still, trembling violently. Lawrence scrambled to his feet, still
holding the bridle, and promptly placed himself
in front of the mare.

For one breathless instant, Lawrence looked
into Fanny's face, and neither spoke nor moved.
Both were still very pale. Then the young girl
slipped off, the reins in her hand.

"That was uncommonly well done," she said,
with great calm. "You've saved my life."

She no longer looked at him while she spoke,
but patted and stroked the thoroughbred, looking
her over with a critical eye.

"Oh — that's all right," answered Lawrence.
" Don't mention it ! "

He laughed nervously, still panting from his

violent exertion. Fanny herself was not out of breath, but the colour did not come back to her sunburnt cheeks at once, and her hand was hardly steady yet. She did not laugh with Lawrence, nor even smile, but she looked long into his eyes.

"I may not mention it, but I shan't forget it," she said slowly.

"It's one to me, isn't it?" asked Lawrence, who, in reality, was by far the cooler and more collected of the two.

"How do you mean?" enquired Fanny, knitting her brows half angrily.

"One to me — in our game, you know," said the young fellow. "The game we agreed to play, yesterday."

"Yes — it's one to you. By the bye — you're not hurt anywhere, are you?"

She looked him over, as she had looked over her mare, with the same critical glance. His clothes were a little torn, here and there, being but light summer things, and his hat had disappeared, but it was tolerably clear that he was in no way injured.

"Oh, I'm all right," he answered cheerfully. "I should think you'd feel badly shaken, though," he added, with sudden anxiety.

"Not at all," said Fanny, determined to show no more emotion or excitement than he. "It was a case of sitting still — neck or nothing. It's nothing, as it happens."

At that moment Brinsley appeared, riding slowly through the trees, for fear of frightening the mare again.

"Are you hurt?" he shouted.

Fanny looked round, saw him, and shook her head, with a smile. Brinsley trotted up and sprang from his horse.

"Are you sure you're not hurt?" he asked again.

"Not in the least!"

"Thank God!" ejaculated Brinsley, with emphasis.

"You'd better thank Mr. Lawrence, too," observed Fanny, quietly. "He caught her going at a gallop, and hung on and was dragged. I don't remember ever seeing anything quite so plucky."

Brinsley looked coldly at his rival, and his beady eyes seemed nearer together than usual when he spoke to him.

" I think you're quite as much to be congratulated as Miss Trehearne," he said.

" Thanks."

" We'd better be getting down to the road again," said Fanny. " You can lead the mare and your own horse, too, Mr. Brinsley. She's quiet enough now, and I've all I can do to walk in these things."

Brinsley took the mare's bridle over her head and led the way with the two horses.

" Aren't you coming?" asked Fanny, seeing that Lawrence did not follow.

" Thanks — no," he answered. " I must find my hat, in the first place."

Brinsley looked over his shoulder, and saw the two hanging back. He stopped a moment, turning, and laying one hand on the mare's nose.

" You must be shaken, Mr. Lawrence," he said. " Why don't you take the groom's horse and ride home with us ? "

" I can't ride," answered the younger man,

loud enough for Brinsley to hear him. "And you know it perfectly well," he added under his breath.

Fanny frowned, but took no further notice of the remark.

"Good-bye," she said, holding out her hand to Lawrence. "Come home as soon as you can, won't you?"

"Oh yes — that is, I think I'll just see you take that fence again, and then I want to get a little higher up the hill and do another bit of a sketch. Then I'll come home. There's no hurry, is there?"

"Don't show off," said Fanny, severely. "It isn't pretty. Good-bye."

She walked fast and overtook Brinsley in a few moments. At the foot of the hill he prepared to mount her, leaving his own horse to the groom. Then a thing happened which he was never able to explain, though he was an expert in the field and no one could mount a lady better than he, of all Fanny's acquaintances. He bent his knee and held out his hand and stiffened his back and made the necessary effort just at the right moment, as he very well knew. But for some inexplicable reason Fanny did not reach the saddle, nor anywhere near it, and she slipped and would certainly have fallen if he had not caught her with his other hand and held her on her feet.

"How awkward you are!" she exclaimed viciously, with a little stamp. "Let me get on alone!"

And thereupon, to his astonishment and mortification, she pushed him aside, set her foot in the stirrup, — for she was very tall and could do it easily, — and was up in a flash. Lawrence, looking down at them from the edge of the woods, saw what had happened, and so did Stebbins, the groom, who grinned in silence. He hated Brinsley, and it is a bad sign when a good servant hates his master's guest. Lawrence felt that in addition to scoring one in the game, he was avenged on his enemy for the latter's taunting invitation to ride.

"I think I may count that, and mark two. I'm sure she did it on purpose," he said audibly to himself.

Before Brinsley was mounted, Fanny was over
the fence with her mare, and waiting for him in
the road.

"Oh, come along!" she cried.   "Don't be all
day getting on!"

"You needn't be so tremendously rough on a
fellow," said Brinsley, as his horse landed in the
road.   "It wasn't my fault that I wasn't waiting
for a runaway under the trees up there."

"Yes it was! Everything's your fault," answered Fanny, emphatically. "No — you needn't play Orlando Furioso and make papa's old rocking-horse waltz like that. My mare's got to walk a mile, at least, for her nerves."

It didn't require Brinsley's great natural penetration to tell him that Miss Fanny Trehearne was in the very worst of tempers — even to the point of unfairly calling her papa's sturdy Hungarian bad names. But he could not at all see why she should be so angry. It had certainly been her fault if he had failed to put her neatly in the saddle. But her ill-humour did not frighten him in the least, though he was very quiet for several minutes after she had last spoken.

"It's not wildly gay to ride with people who don't talk," observed Fanny.

"I was trying to think of something appropriate to say," answered Brinsley. "But you're in such an awful rage — "

"Am I? I didn't know it. What makes you think so?"

"What nerves you've got!" exclaimed Brinsley, in a tone of admiration.

"I haven't any nerves at all."

"I mean good nerves."

"I tell you I haven't any nerves. Why do you talk about nerves? They're not amusing things to have, are they?"

"Well — in point of humour — I didn't say they were."

"I asked you to say something amusing, and you began talking about nerves," said Fanny, in explanation.

"I'm not in luck to-day," said Brinsley, after a pause.

"No — you're not," was the answer; but she did not vouchsafe him a glance.

"I wish you'd like me," he said boldly.

"I do — at a certain distance. You look well in the landscape — and you know it."

"Upon my word!" Brinsley laughed roughly, and looked between his horse's ears.

"Upon your word — what?"

"I never had anything said to me quite equal to that, Miss Trehearne."

"No? I'm surprised. Perhaps you haven't known the right sort of people. You must find the truth refreshing."

Brinsley waited a few moments before speaking, and then, turning his head, looked at her with great earnestness.

" I wish you'd tell me why you've taken such a sudden dislike to me," he said in a low voice.

" Why are you so anxious to know, Mr. Brinsley?" asked Fanny, meeting his eyes quietly.

" Because I believe that somebody has been saying disagreeable things about me to you," he answered. " If that's the case, it would be fair to give me a chance, you know."

" Nobody's been talking against you. You've talked against yourself. Besides," she added, her face suddenly clearing, " it's quite absurd to make such a fuss about nothing! I'm only angry about nothing at all. It's my way, you know. You mustn't mind. I'll get over it before we're at home, and then I'll go off, and my cousins will give you lots of weak tea and flattery."

Brinsley, who was clever at most things, was not good at talking nor at understanding a woman's moods, and he felt himself at so great a disadvantage that he slipped into an inane

conversation about people and parties without
succeeding in finding out what he wished to
know. If he had ever conceived any mad hope
of winning Fanny's affections, he abandoned it
then and there. He was still further handi-
capped, had Fanny known it, by the desperate
state of his own affairs at that moment; and if
she had known something of his reflexions, she
might have pitied him a little — what she might
have thought, if she had guessed the remainder,
is hard to guess, for he had a very curious
scheme in his mind for improving his finances.
He had been playing high for some time, had
lost steadily, and was at the end of his present
resources, which, with him, meant that he was
at the end of all he had in the world.

He was not by any means inclined to give up
the pleasant intimacy he had formed and fostered
with the three Miss Miners, nor the attendant
luxuries which he had gained with it, and the
introduction to Bar Harbour society, which
meant good society elsewhere. But he felt that
he had no choice, since the cards went against
him. He was not a sharper. He played fair, for

the sake of the enjoyment of the thing. It was his one great passion. When he was in luck he won enough for his extravagant needs, for he always played high, on principle. But when fortune foiled him, he had other talents of a more curious description, by the exercise of which to replenish his purse — talents, too, which he had exercised in America for a long time. His happy hunting-ground was really London, which accounted for his evident and almost extraordinary familiarity with its ways. There are indeed few places in the world where a man may follow a doubtful occupation more freely and more successfully.

Before they reached the Trehearnes' house, Brinsley had made up his mind that he must drink his last cup of tea with the three Miss Miners on that day or very soon afterwards, unless he were to be even more fortunate in his undertaking than he dared to expect. The immediate consequence was an affectation of a sad and stately manner towards Fanny as he helped her off her mare at the door.

"I'm afraid this has been our last ride," he said, in a subdued voice.

"What? Oh — 'The Last Ride' — Browning — I remember," answered Fanny.

"No — I wasn't alluding to Browning. I'm going away very soon."

Fanny stared at him in some surprise.

"Oh! Are you? I am very sorry." She spoke cheerfully, and led the way into the house, Brinsley following her, with a dejected air. "You'll probably find my cousins in the library," she added. "I'm going to take off my hat — it's so hot."

The three Miss Miners were assembled, as usual at that hour, and greeted Brinsley effusively. Not wishing to be anticipated by Fanny in telling a story altogether to Lawrence's credit, he began to tell the three ladies of what had happened during the ride. He was very careful to explain that he had of course not dared to follow the runaway, lest he should have made matters much worse.

"It's quite dreadful," cried Miss Cordelia, on hearing of Fanny's narrow escape. "You should never have let her jump the fence at all. What do people do such mad things for!"

" If anything happened to the child, we might as well kill ourselves," said Elizabeth. " It's too dreadful to think of ! "

" Well," answered Brinsley, " nothing has happened, you see. I've brought Miss Trehearne safe home, though I hadn't the good fortune to be the man who stopped her horse. You see," he added, smiling, " I want all the credit you can spare from Mr. Lawrence. I'm afraid there's not much to be got, though. He's had the lion's share."

" And where is he ? " asked Augusta, who felt more sympathy for the artist than the others.

" Oh — he'll come back. He can't ride, you know, so he had to walk, poor fellow! He'd been pretty badly shaken, too, and he's not strong, I'm sure."

" You wouldn't have called him weak if you'd seen him hanging on while the mare dragged him," said Fanny, who had entered unnoticed.

" Oh, that's only strength in the hands ! " said Brinsley, in a depreciative tone, and conscious of his own splendid proportions.

o

"Well, then, he's strong in the hands, that's all," retorted Fanny. "Please, some tea, Elizabeth dear — I'm half dead."

The three Miss Miners did their best to console Brinsley for Fanny's continued ill-treatment of him, but they did not succeed in lifting the cloud from his brow. At last he confessed that he was expecting to leave Bar Harbour at any moment.

CHAPTER XI.

THERE were to be fireworks that evening at the Canoe Club on the farther side of Bar Island — magnificent fireworks, it was said, which it would be well worth while to see. The night was calm and clear, and the moon, being near the last quarter, would not rise until everything was over.

"We'll go in skiffs," said Fanny. "When we're tired of each other, we can change about, you know. Mr. Lawrence can take one of us and Mr. Brinsley another, and the other two must take one of the men from the landing. I ordered the boats this morning when I was out."

The three Miss Miners looked consciously at

one another, mutely wondering how they were to
divide Mr. Brinsley amongst them, and wishing
that they had consulted together in private before the moment for decision had come. But no
one suggested that, as there were only four ladies,
each of the men could very easily take two in a
boat.

"We might toss up to see who shall take
whom," suggested Brinsley, who had been un-
usually silent during the greater part of dinner.

"In how many ways can you arrange six people in couples?" asked Fanny.

Nobody succeeded in solving the question, of
course. Even Elizabeth Miner, who was considered the clever member, gave it up in despair.

"Never mind!" said Fanny. "We'll see how
it turns out when we get down to the landing-
stage. These things always arrange themselves."

To the surprise of every one except Fanny herself, the arrangement turned out to be such that
she and Miss Cordelia went together in the skiff
pulled by the sailor, while Brinsley and Lawrence
each took one of the other Miss Miners.

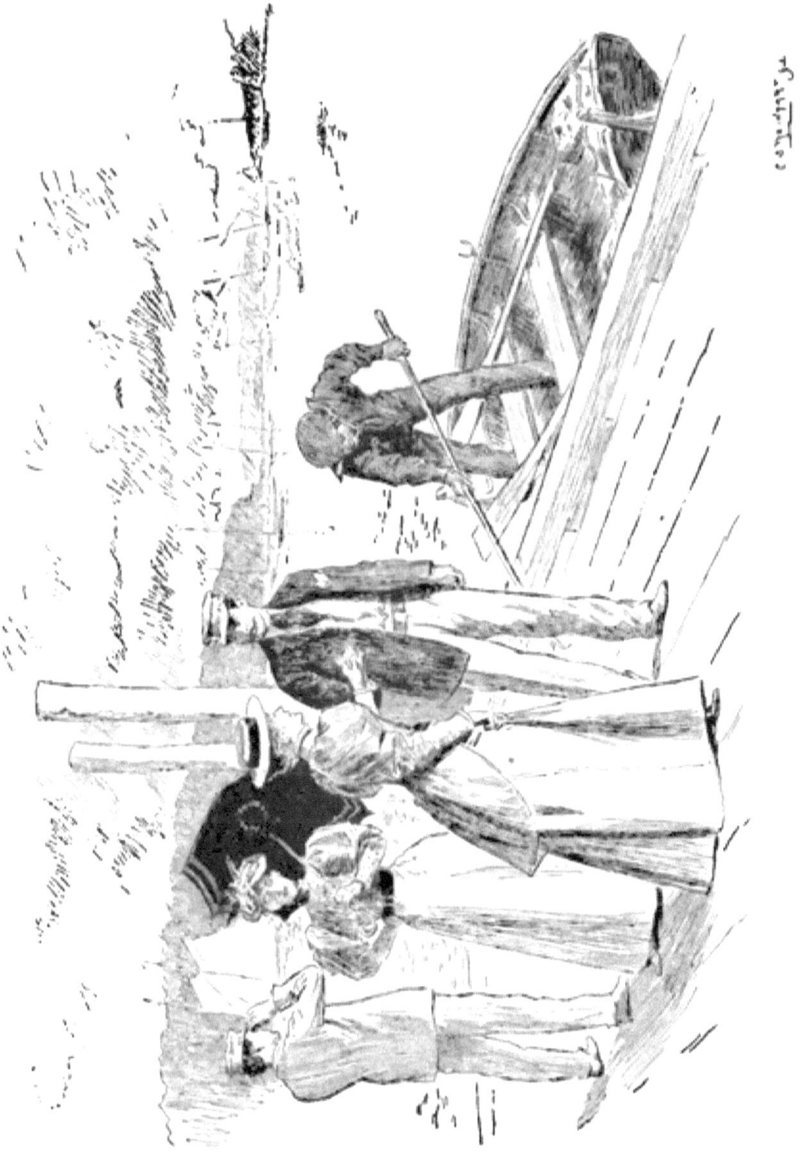

" We'll change by and by," said Fanny, as her boat shoved off first to show the way. " Keep close to us in the crowd when we get over."

The distance from the landing, across the harbour, through the channel between Bar Island and Sheep Porcupine to the Canoe Club, is little over half a mile; but at night, amidst a crowd of steamers, large and small, row-boats, canoes, and sail-boats, — the latter all outside the channel, — it took twenty minutes to reach the place where the fireworks were to be.

Fanny leaned back beside her cousin, and watched the lights in silence. Yellow, green, and red, they streamed across the brilliant black water in every direction, the yellow rays fixed or moving but slowly, the others gliding along swiftly above their own reflection, as the paddle steamers thrashed their way through the still sea. To left and right the shadowy islands loomed darkly against the black sky, outlined by the stars. The warm damp air lifted the coolness from the water in little puffs, as the skiff slipped along. Now and then, in the gloom, a boat showed dimly alongside, and the laughing voices of girls and

boys told how near it passed, a mere floating
dimness upon blackness. The stroke of light
sculls swished and tinkled with the laughter.
The soft mysterious charm of the summer dark
was breathed upon land and water — the distant
lights were love-dreaming eyes, and each time, as
the oars dipped, swept and rose, the gentle sound
was like a stolen kiss.

Then, suddenly, with a wild screaming rush,
a rocket shot up into the night, splitting the sky
with a scar of fire. The burning point of it
lingered a moment overhead, then cracked into
little stars that shed a soft glow through the
gloom, and fell in a swift shower of sparks.
Then all was hushed again, and the red and
green lights moved quickly over the water,
hither and thither.

Close to the shore of the island the skiff ran
round the point into the shallow water along the
beach, and all at once in the distance the festooned lanterns of the Canoe Club came into
view, so bright that one could distinguish the
branches of the spruces in the red and yellow
glare, and the moving crowd of people on the

Canoe Club.

little landing-stage and below, before the club-house. And some two hundred yards out, the lights began again, gleaming from hundreds of boats and little vessels of all rigs and builds. Between these seaward lights and those on land a deep black void stretched away up French-man's Bay.

Miss Cordelia started nervously at the rockets, but said nothing. Fanny sat beside her in silence. The sailor, only visible distinctly when the lights were behind him, pulled softly and steadily, glancing over his shoulder every now and then to see that the way was clear. The other skiffs kept near, both Brinsley and Law-rence being keenly on the lookout for a change. Now and then Fanny could hear them talking.

" I wonder why one voice should attract one and another should be disagreeable," she said at last, in a meditative tone.

" I was thinking of the same thing," answered Cordelia, thoughtfully.

"Yes," said Fanny, absently. "Of course you were," she added, a moment later. " I mean—" She paused. " Poor dear!" she exclaimed at

last, stroking her cousin's elderly hand in the
dark. " I'm so sorry ! "

" Thank you, dear," answered Miss Miner, simply and gratefully.

It was little enough, but little as it was it made
them both more silent than ever. With the boat-
man close before them, it was impossible to talk
of what was in their thoughts. Fanny, for her
part, was glad of it. She had understood her
old-maid cousin since the night when Cordelia
had broken down and laughed and cried in the
garden, and she knew how little there could be
to say. But Cordelia did not understand Fanny
in the least. It was a marvel to her that any one
should prefer Lawrence to Brinsley — almost as
great a marvel as that she herself, in her sober
middle age, should have felt what she knew was
love and believed to be passion.

And now, Brinsley was going, and it was over.
He would never come back, and she should never
see him again — she was sure of that, she was
only an old maid ; a middle-aged gentlewoman
who had never possessed any great attraction for
anybody ; who had always been more or less poor

and unhappy, though of the best and living amongst the best; whose few pleasures had come to her unexpectedly, like rare gleams of pale sunshine on a very long rainy day; who had looked for little and had got next to nothing out of life, save the crumbs of enjoyment from the feast of rich relations, like the Trehearnes — a woman who had known something more grievous than sorrow and worse than violent grief, trudging through life in the leaden cowl of many limitations — the leaden cowl of that most innocent of all hypocrites, of her, or of him, who knows the daily burden of keeping up appearances on next to nothing, and of doctoring poor little illusions through a feeble existence, worth having because they represent all that there is to have.

She had been wounded by one of those arrows shot in the dark which hit hearts unawares and unaimed; and now that the shaft was suddenly drawn out, the heart's blood followed it and the nerves quivered where it had been. It was only one of the little tragedies which no one sees, few guess at, and nothing can hinder. But Fanny Trehearne felt that it was beside her, there in the little boat, while she watched the pretty fireworks, and she was sorry and did what she could to soothe the pain.

" Let's change, now," she said at last, just as the glow of a multitude of coloured fires died away on the water. " You take Mr. Brinsley, and I'll take Mr. Lawrence."

As she spoke, she gave her cousin's hand a little squeeze of sympathy, and heard the small sigh of satisfaction that answered the proposal. The re-arrangement was effected in a few moments, the men holding the boats together by the gunwales while the ladies stepped from one into the other.

" Pull away," said Fanny, authoritatively, as soon as Lawrence had shoved off. " Let's get out of this! I'll steer, so you needn't bother about running into things."

Fairly seated in a boat, with the sculls shipped, and some one at the tiller lines, Lawrence could get along tolerably well, for he knew just enough not to catch a crab in smooth water, so long as he was not obliged to turn his head. But if he had to look over his shoulder, something was certain to happen, which was natural, considering that when he attempted to feather at all, he did it the wrong way.

"You're stronger than anybody would think," observed Fanny, as she saw how quickly the skiff moved. "You might do things quite decently, if you'd only take the trouble to learn."

"Oh no! I'm a born duffer," laughed Lawrence. "Besides, I couldn't row long like this. I couldn't keep it up."

They were just in front of the club-house now; and a score of rockets went up together, with a rushing and a crackling and a gleaming, as they soared and burst, and at last fell sputtering in the water all around the skiff. Lawrence had rested on his sculls to watch the sight.

"Pull away!" said Fanny. "We'll get under the foot-bridge by the landing. There's water enough there, and we can see everything."

Lawrence obeyed, and pulled as hard as he could.

"So your friend Mr. Brinsley is going away," observed the young girl, suddenly.

"My friend! I like that! As though I had brought him in my pocket."

"I'm very glad that he's going, at all events," said Fanny, without heeding his remark. "I'm not fond of him any more."

"I hope you never were — fond of him."

"Oh yes, I was — but I'm thankful to say that it's over. Of all the ineffable cads! I could have killed him to-day!"

"By the bye," said Lawrence, "when he was mounting you — didn't you do that on purpose?"

"Of course. And then I called him awkward. It was so nice! It did me good."

"Pure spite, I suppose. You couldn't have had any particular reason for doing it, could you?"

"Oh dear, no! What reason could I have? It wasn't his fault that the mare ran away, though I told him it was."

"That's interesting," observed Lawrence. "Do you often do things out of pure spite?"

"Constantly — without any reason at all!" Fanny laughed.

"Perhaps you'll marry out of spite, some day," said Lawrence, calmly. "Women often do, they say, though I never could understand why."

"I daresay I shall. I'm quite capable of it. And shouldn't I be just horrid afterwards!"

"I like you when you're horrid, as you call it. I didn't at first. You've given my sense of humour a chance to grow since I've been here. I say, Miss Trehearne—" He stopped.

"What do you say? It isn't particularly polite to begin in that way, is it? I suppose it's English."

"Oh, bother the English! And I apologize for being slangy. It's so dark that I can't see you frown. I meant to say, if you ever marry out of spite, and want to be particularly horrid afterwards, it wouldn't be a bad idea to marry me, for I don't mind that sort of thing a bit, you know."

"That's a singular offer!" laughed Fanny, leaning far back, and playing with the tiller lines in the glow of the Bengal lights.

"It's genuine of its kind," answered the young man. "Of course it isn't a sure thing, exactly," he added reflectively, "because it depends on your happening to be in the spiteful humour. But, as you say that often happens—"

"Well, go on!"

P

" I thought you might feel spiteful enough to accept this evening," concluded Lawrence.

" Take care — I might, you know — you're in danger!" She was still laughing.

"Don't mind me, you know! I could stand it, I believe."

"You're awfully amusing — sometimes, Mr. Lawrence."

" Meaning now?" enquired the artist, resting on his sculls, for they were under the shadow of the bridge.

" I can't see your face distinctly," answered Fanny. "So much depends on the expression. But I think —"

" What do you think? That it's awfully amusing of me to offer to be married as a sacrifice, to your spite?"

" It's amusing anyway."

" A formal proposal would be, you mean?" asked Lawrence. Then he laughed oddly.

" I hate formality," answered Fanny. "That is, in earnest, you know. It's so disgusting when a man comes with his gloves buttoned and sits on the edge of a chair and says —"

" And say what ? "

" Oh — you know the sort of thing. You must have done it scores of times."

" What? Proposed and been refused? You're complimentary, at all events. I've a great mind to let you be the first, just — well — how shall

I say? Just to associate you with a novel sensation."

"I might disappoint you," said Fanny, demurely. "I told you so before. Just think, if I were to say 'yes,' you'd be most dreadfully caught. You'd have to eat humble pie and beg off, and say that you hadn't meant it."

"Oh no!" laughed the young man. "You'd break it off in a week, and then it would be all right."

"Are you going to be rude? Or are you, already? I'm not quite sure."

"Neither. Of course you'd break it off, if we had an agreement to that effect."

"You don't make any allowance for my spitefulness. It would be just like me to hold you to your engagement. Of course you wouldn't live long. We should be sure to fight."

"Oh — sure," assented Lawrence. "That is, if you call this fighting."

"It would be worse than this. But why don't you try? I'm dying to refuse you. I'm just in the humour."

"Why! I thought you said there was danger!

Channel between Bar Island and Sheep Porcupine.

If I'd known there wasn't — by the bye, this counts in the game, doesn't it?"

"There isn't anything to count, yet," said Fanny. "Look at those fiery fish — aren't they pretty? See how they squirm about, and fizzle, and behave like mad things! Oh, I never saw anything so pretty as that!"

"Yes. If one must have an interruption, they do as well as anything."

"You weren't talking very coherently, I believe," said the young girl, turning her head to watch the fireworks. "And you've made me miss lots of pretty things, I'm sure. Oh — they've gone out already! How dark it seems, all at once! What were you asking? Whether this counted in the game? Of course it counts. Everything does. But I don't exactly see how —"

She stopped and looked towards him in the dim gloom of the shadow under the bridge. But Lawrence did not speak. He looked over the side of the boat, softly slapping the black water with the blade of his scull.

"Why don't you go on?" asked Fanny, tap-

ping the boards under her foot to attract his
attention.

"I was thinking over the proper words,"
answered Lawrence. "How does one make a
formal proposal of marriage? I never did such
a thing in my life."

"An informal one would do for fun."

"I never did that, either."

"Never?"

"Never."

"Really? Swear it, as they say on the stage."
Fanny laughed softly.

"Oh, by Jove, yes!" answered Lawrence,
promptly. "I'll swear to that by anything you
please."

"Well — you'll have to do it some day, so
you'd better practise at once," suggested Fanny.

Lawrence did not notice that there was a
sort of little relief in her tone.

"I suppose one says, 'My angel, will you
be mine?'" he said. "That sounds like some
book or other."

"It might do," answered Fanny, meditatively.
"You ought to throw a little more expression

into the tone. Besides, I'm not an angel, whatever the girl in the book may have been. On the whole — no — it's a little too effusive. Angel — you know. It's such nonsense! Try something else; but put lots of expression into it."

" Does one get down on one's knees ? " enquired Lawrence.

"Oh no; I don't believe it's necessary. Besides, you'd upset the boat."

" All right — here goes! My dear Miss Trehearne, will you — "

" Yes. That's it. Go on. The quaver in the voice is rather well done. 'Will you — ' What ? "

" Will you marry me ? "

" Yes, Mr. Lawrence, I will."

There was a short pause, during which a number of fiery fish were sent off again, and squirmed and wriggled and fizzled their burning little lives away in the water. But neither of the young people looked at them.

" You rather took my breath away," said Lawrence, with a change of tone. " Did I do it all right ? "

"Oh — quite right," answered Fanny, thoughtfully.

Immediately after the words Lawrence heard a little sigh. Then Fanny heard one, too.

"You didn't happen to be in earnest, did you?" she asked suddenly, in a low, soft voice.

"Well — I didn't mean — that I meant — you know we agreed to play a game —"

"I know we did — but — were you in earnest?"

"Yes — but, of course — Oh, this isn't fair, Miss Trehearne!"

"Yes, it is. I said 'yes,' didn't I?"

"Certainly, but —"

"There's no 'but.' I happened to be in earnest, too — that's all. I've lost the game."

www.ingramcontent.com/pod-product-compliance
Lightning Source LLC
Chambersburg PA
CBHW030128030726
47498CB00007B/2605